VOW TO DEFEND

A FLYING CROSS RANCH ROMANCE
BOOK SIX

SHANAE JOHNSON

THOSE JOHNSON GIRLS

CHAPTER ONE

"Your mama is so old, she took her driving test on a triceratops."

A chorus of oohs rang up in the backyard of the Bright Horizon's Foster Home. The sun was setting on the horizon as Aldo Gonzalez jutted out his chin and peered down at his domain as all the foster kids, young and older, cheered his opening entry in the game of Dirty Dozens.

Aldo was faced off against the new kid. Christopher, or Topher as he told everyone to call him, was bigger than Aldo. Which was why Aldo had immediately challenged him. He'd known better than to use his fists, too. With those steak-sized hands, Topher could pound him into the ground. But no one could best Aldo's mouth.

"Your mama is so fat..." Topher fidgeted, those meat-sized hands grinding one into the other like he was pounding pizza dough.

The thought of pizza made Aldo's belly grumble. They'd already had a cold breakfast of runny oatmeal and a lunch of crunchy chicken nuggets and oily fries. Dinner wouldn't be for another four hours. During the summer months, Aldo wished for school because then at least he could sneak into the cafeteria at a different lunch period and grab seconds, and sometimes thirds.

"No, your mama is ugly..."

The kids around them were already snickering and pointing. Topher hadn't even gotten out a full sentence, and he'd already lost this game. This was the only game that mattered in the foster system. Even at the young age of twelve, Aldo had learned this lesson quickly. If you're not high up on the food chain, you might not eat.

Because Aldo was at the top, kids gave him an extra cookie, or an extra juice box in order to get favors from him. Or to keep him from challenging them to a game of the Dirty Dozens where Aldo would humiliate them.

"Your mama… your mama is…"

Aldo began to snicker. You might be the biggest or meanest on the playground, but laughing at a kid would always point out that they were the loser. All around, the other kids began to laugh. A few pointed at Topher. The bear cub of a boy pursed his lips. They began to tremble. Aldo knew that if the boy cried, he would never live it down, and Aldo would retain his place as king of the backyard of foster care.

"Yeah, well, you don't have a mother," Topher said. "At least I do."

It was never silent in a foster home. There was always someone shouting, be it child or adult. There was always someone crying, either in pain or from hunger. There was always some sound of human misery. But there was never silence.

Every mouth shut at Topher's words. Even the birds in the trees hushed in anticipation of what Aldo would do. Even the insects on the ground stopped the search of scraps to see what would happen next.

It had been a long time since Aldo had had an actual challenge. The comeback blindsided him. Over Topher's shoulder, Aldo saw his reflection.

A kid just his height, with his same coloring

and facial expressions, broke off from the crowd. Aldo's mirror image was calm and unassuming. His double kept his hands in his pockets, his shoulders hunched as though telling Aldo that he should concede the fight.

Aldo ignored his twin brother. Instead of lifting his fists, Aldo opened his mouth. "Yeah, but you were so ugly your mom put you here so she didn't have to look at you anymore."

Topher's head snapped back. If Aldo had actually struck the boy, the crack of the muscles in his neck wouldn't have been so loud. Those meat fists stopped grinding and formed two huge cleavers. The cleavers rose and flew.

Aldo saw the blow coming. He was fast enough to duck away. Topher's knuckles only grazed his ear. But when Aldo blinked, he saw red.

Not blood. He saw red hair. He saw the biggest green eyes he'd ever seen. The contrast was so striking to him that he didn't immediately put up his guard, and Topher got in a free punch.

When the ringing in Aldo's head stopped and he blinked, he was seeing double. Two heads of red hair. They looked similar, much like he and his brother looked similar. But Aldo could tell the two girls apart.

Another set of twins. Someone else like him and Mateo. He wondered if they had lost their parents like he had. Or if their parents had given them up like a lot of kids here had.

Aldo opened his mouth to ask her, but the redhead cringed and turned away from him. Confusion was Aldo's first reaction. Pain was his second as Topher's fist landed in his gut, nearly forcing Aldo to give back the nuggets and fries from lunch.

"That's enough." Mateo stepped in between Aldo and the blond bear cub.

There was a part of Aldo that knew he had to get up and deal with Topher. He'd taken two blows with no retaliation. His street cred had taken a hit along with his body. But his eyes went again to the redhead.

She was looking at him again. Her arm was around her twin. The other girl had her face buried in her neck. His twin, the one with the fire in her green eyes, looked down her nose at Aldo.

A few of the girls at school looked at Aldo with stupid grins on their faces, and he hated it. If he tried to play the Dirty Dozens with any of them, they'd tear up. He doubted this girl would. She looked like the type that would challenge him right back.

Aldo climbed to his feet. He started toward the redhead, but a hand held him back.

"I said that's enough."

Aldo blinked at Mateo. His brother stood with both his hands outstretched. One was on Aldo's heaving chest. The other was on Topher's.

But Aldo had completely forgotten about the other kid. He didn't care what the other kids might think of him now that Topher had gotten in two blows, and Mateo had to step in to help Aldo. The only opinion he cared about was the redhead's.

His redhead's attention was still on her twin. When the other girl lifted her head and chanced a glance over at him, Aldo heard Mateo exhale. His hand dropped from Aldo's chest as he turned and stared at the newcomers.

Aldo knew what Mateo was experiencing. They had that twin sense, after all. Neither of them had ever seen a girl with red hair before. It was like their mother's favorite doll. The doll Mateo sometimes took out of their garbage bag of belongings and held close to his chest when Aldo felt that hollow ache in his chest from missing his mother.

Aldo had never needed to do that. He wouldn't

be caught dead with a doll. But he had fought when another kid had tried to steal it from Mateo. Both he and Mateo had gotten punished for that. But now he was seeing a living and breathing Raggedy Ann and Andy dolls. She wasn't ugly like his mother's dolls. Probably because her eyes weren't made of buttons. They were as green as the fields he liked to run in.

The girls turned and were walking away from the clearing in the yard, along with the other foster kids. In wordless agreement, Aldo and Mateo took a step to follow them.

"You two stay out of my way," snarled Topher from behind them.

Neither Aldo nor Mateo turned to acknowledge him. Together, they could've taken the kid. Mateo definitely could've, but Mateo preferred to keep both his words and his fists to himself. But it was Mateo who spoke first.

"Hello," Mateo called out.

Neither girl stopped walking, though Aldo was certain they'd heard Mateo's greeting. The first one, Aldo's twin, turned back, flashing green fire at him.

The heat in her gaze made something flutter in his belly. His heart did a weird skip, like it fell down. When it got back up and he gulped down air to fill his lungs, Aldo said the first thing that came to his mind.

"Hey... red," he said.

They both stopped. The smaller one cowered away from him. They were both the same height. But Aldo's twin seemed somehow bigger. Once again, she flashed those green eyes at him.

Aldo's heart did that same weird skip. His belly made the sound of being empty and in need. But looking at her, he didn't feel in the least bit hungry. He felt like he could get his fill just by staring at her.

"That's offensive," she said.

Aldo liked the way her lips moved when she formed words. English hadn't been his first language. He'd learned by watching people form the words. Her voice, her words, were smooth and clear.

"We're not interested in playing your childish game," she said. "We might be new here, but we don't need you making fun of us."

But he wasn't making fun. He hadn't mentioned her mother at all. He'd only said hello. And mentioned the color of her hair. Because he didn't know what else to say to her.

"You're nothing but a bully, and I don't want anything to do with you."

And with that, she turned. Those green eyes flashed again. Those lips moved in a way that made his chest tighten. And that hair flung around.

Mateo sighed and watched the girls walk off without any objection. Aldo made to follow, but Mateo held him back.

"Leave them alone," said his brother.

Aldo didn't follow them, but he had no intention of leaving her alone. He wanted to see her eyes flash that green fire again. He wanted to watch her lips move in that precise way. He wanted his belly to feel full, like it did when he had her attention. He'd just have to wait another day to get his fill of her.

CHAPTER TWO

Elayne Jade had suffered from migraines since puberty. The headaches came on when she was stressed. Or when she ate too much sugar. And also during the rare times when she'd had one too many drinks.

She was stressed. She remembered that much. Her job as a school guidance counselor had been her dream since her first Career Day in middle school. Now that she was in the counseling suite in the halls of her alma mater, the politics of the position had been tying her in knots for the last few years.

That stress had driven her to keep chocolate candies in her purse. She'd filled up the belly of her bag for the weekend she'd spent at a counseling conference. She had the distinct memory of reaching for one of the foil-wrapped stressbusters at the end of the conference yesterday, and she'd come away empty-handed.

So two out of three of her nemesis had tackled her. Or was it nemeses? Nemesi?

It hurt her brain to try to be smart this morning. Not when it was doing karate kicks against her cranium. Wait? Was the cranium at the front or the back?

The devil if she knew. When she tried to sit up, it felt like a devil was sitting on her chest. Elayne winced, causing her brows to press together, her nose to wrinkle, and her tongue to press against the roof of her mouth. That's when she tasted it.

Last night she'd sat at the bar. She distinctly remembered the curly-haired blond handing her a drink. But the drink hadn't been clear liquid. It had been darker. But not quite amber.

Elayne forced her brain to pull up a coherent picture of last night, but it was all hazy. The dark drink was the only thing she could make out. It hadn't reflected the light like a normal dark-colored liquor. It had been thicker. And sugary. With a hint of bitterness. Kinda like…

Had she had a chocolate drink? The bittersweet remnants in her mouth confirmed her suspicions.

Wait? Had she ordered a second? And then... was that a third drink she was remembering?

The pounding on the right side of her head suggested she had finished all three. The throbbing on the left side of her face felt like it had rested against an anvil. The pins pricking at the back of her skull felt like the hammer was still pounding. The silence was so loud it made her ears ring.

Was she outside? She swore she heard running water. And was that singing? Was the radio on?

It had to be the radio because her sister's voice was not that low. But wait? Kailyn liked instrumental music and not vocalists. Also, Kailyn's bedroom was down the hall with her own private en suite. Elayne shouldn't be hearing her twin's voice or radio.

And why were her curtains closed? Elayne's room was at the back of their house. She always slept with the curtains opened and the windows cracked. The sunrise and birds chirping had been her natural alarm clock since she and her sister had moved into their adoptive parents' home.

There was no birdsong this morning. There

was only that loud, ringing silence. And the man's voice coming from the bathroom.

But wait. Had she left the conference hotel yet? She had no memory of it. Just as she had no memory of what had happened after that third drink.

She wasn't home. She was still in the hotel. That much helped her get a bearing on her whereabouts and ground her in space and time.

Her blurry weekend started to come into focus. She'd arrived at the Purple Heart Ranch on Friday for a workshop for school counselors to learn more about how the veterans on the ranch were working with disadvantaged youth. Elayne remembered the wizened face of Dr. Patel, a leading psychologist who worked with wounded veterans. Those vets had brought kids onto their rehabilitation ranch and begun using the same healing techniques prized for healing their battle wounds with adolescents and teenagers to great effect.

Elayne had taken many notes, which was why her hands were sore. She had ridden a horse, which was why her legs ached a bit. That didn't explain why she had gone and had not one, not two, but three drinks at the bar two nights later.

Saturday was a bit clearer. She'd taken a seat at the front of the conference room, eager to share her ideas with the other guidance counselors from around the state. At every turn, she'd been silenced, talked over, or outright ignored by the gray-haired men and diamond ring-wearing women.

Elayne's hair was a vibrant red. Her fingers were bare of jewels. She was the youngest person in the room and unmarried. For that reason, the counselors made no secret that they thought she should sit quietly at the back and let them steer the guiding.

The ageism of it all curled her hands into fists. The notion that vows trumped her degrees and experience made her lip curl. But it was the sound of the water in the bathroom stopping that made her stomach drop.

Shifting on the bed, trying not to make a sound, Elayne had a moment of gratification when she saw that beneath the covers she was still clothed. Mostly.

Her shoes were off. Her blouse hung over the back of a chair. There was a cotton cami covering her chest and belly. Her skirt, though wrinkled, was still on and zipped up.

Relief swam through Elayne to know that nothing had happened under the sheets last night. But still there was a man in her bathroom.

Elayne was not the type of girl that got caught up in a one-night stand. She'd only had two boyfriends in her entire life, and neither relationship had progressed to weekends away in hotel rooms. Definitely not with her high school boyfriend Darius Cox, which had only lasted a couple of weeks before he'd broken up with her over text. Elayne had no idea, no memory, no inkling of who could be behind that door.

Rolling over, she saw that there was a head imprint on the pillow beside her. The sheets next to her were ruffled. Had he slept here? In her room? In her bed?

The mystery man shuffled behind the closed bathroom door. Were those the sounds of a strange man getting dressed? Was he on his way out? Elayne had to get away from here.

Her feet slapped down onto the thick carpet. Her head protested the shift from horizontal to vertical. The ringing started up in her ears again. So too did the singing.

Elayne stopped moving. Her head cleared. Not enough that she remembered every detail of last night. No, her head remembered the first time she'd heard that song.

The man in the bathroom was singing Bruce Springsteen's "Red-Headed Woman."

The lines of that song had been explicit for a twelve-year-old kid to know. They were even more racy coming from that same foul mouth in his late twenties. What was she doing in the same hotel room as Aldo Matthews?

Not just the same room but the same bed? What possible reason would she have had to let Aldo into her room? If that was his head indent on the pillow, had the world outside come to an end with pigs flying around on angel's wings?

A look out the window showed a bright, sunny day. Cars zoomed by in the distance. The only thing in the sky was a Boeing 747 taking off in the distance.

Elayne ran a hand down her face. Something cold touched her forehead, giving her a moment of relief. Her eyes locked on the ring on her lefthand finger. Her head stopped pounding for a second as shock took over her system.

What was that ring doing on her finger?

The door to the bathroom opened. Aldo was framed in the doorway. And he was... smiling.

Elayne had never seen the man smile. Definitely not at her. The look scrambled her brain even more. And then he opened his mouth, and her world tilted off its axis.

"There's my beautiful bride," he said. "How'd you sleep?"

CHAPTER THREE

Aldo joined the chorus of feet tapping on the sticky linoleum flooring of the history class. All eyes weren't on Mr. Merchant, who droned on at the head of the class. The middle schoolers' gazes were on the clock on the wall, watching the seconds tick by. Just a few more rotations and they'd all be set free for recess.

Recess and lunch were the only reasons Aldo enjoyed school. He was good at math, but bored by it. He was bored by history, but good at memorizing all the facts. Studying any subject seemed like a waste of time to him, since he knew exactly what he'd be doing when he turned eighteen.

Like his adoptive father, Aldo would be enlisting and joining the United States Air Force.

The military had made a fine man of his father. Aldo's only goal in the world was to be exactly like Haran Matthews when he grew up. School was just a way to pass the time until his real life could begin.

Aldo would much rather be back at the Flying Cross Ranch doing his chores and taking care of the animals. Father Matthews gave him and his brothers a lot of responsibilities. Aldo now had four other brothers. One of them was Topher, who had gotten a lot better at the Dozens now that he and Aldo shared the same last name.

Unlike his actual blood brother, Topher liked to get into scraps and fights. While Mateo always had Aldo's back, Topher was usually the one to actually back Aldo up in any skirmish. Mateo was always looking far off in the distance, like he was waiting for someone to show up.

Finally, the fifth period bell rang. Aldo held fast to his seat. His knuckles were white from gripping the underside of the chair. His adoptive mother had drilled manners into him. Aldo knew he wasn't actually dismissed until the adult in the room said so.

"Enjoy your recess, children."

Aldo hated being called a child. He'd had to do

more things than most grownups before he was ten years old. He'd buried both his parents. Had to take care of himself and his brother in the foster care system. And now he had grown man chores on the farm at the ranch. Because he loved his adopted parents and knew you never talked back to adults, he held his tongue as he rose from his desk.

"Let's head to the basketball court before the others get there," he said to Mateo.

The middle school administrators had originally put Aldo and Mateo in separate classes their first month of sixth grade. Something or other about how the research proved that twins did better when they had separate experiences. People were always saying that about him and his brother. But none of the people talking were twins themselves.

Aldo had originally been in Ms. Frances's history class. After raising his hand every three minutes and asking question after question, Ms. Frances's patience visibly began to wear thin. Apparently, there was such a thing as a stupid question, and Aldo knew how to ask them all with a straight, inquiring face. Mateo had been staring out the window on the day Aldo had surprised him in Mr. Merchant's class. For some reason, his twin hadn't been pleased to see him. Then Aldo glanced at the seats near the window and saw the reason why. Kailyn Jade was in the class.

There were three sets of twins in the town. The Silver twins, Gunny and Tilly, who were a couple of years younger than Aldo and Mateo. And the Jade twins, who were the same age as the Matthews twins.

Elayne Jade had made it known that Aldo was her nemesis. He'd had to look that word up in the dictionary. A nemesis was the agent of someone's downfall. Like the villain in a superhero movie. Except there was a secondary definition beneath the first. The second definition said the nemesis was a goddess.

That was Elayne Jade: a red-haired goddess. It was her mission to bring Aldo to his knees. Well, all he had to say to that was bring it on.

Which meant that having Kailyn Jade, the nemesis' sister, in their history class might prove a problem. So of course, Mateo was worried about any recon the sidekick could bring back to her sister. But Kailyn mostly kept quiet, often doodling in her book. She didn't even look up at Aldo when he came into the room.

"I have an extra credit assignment to do," Mateo was saying in response to Aldo's recess plans.

Aldo wracked his brains to figure out what assignment they had that they hadn't finished. He and his brother were in almost every class together. Except art class. No matter how hard he tried, Aldo couldn't talk Mateo into ditching the crayon class and taking another gym class with him.

"Do it later," said Aldo.

"I won't have time. We have soccer practice later."

"Fine," Aldo huffed. "I'll come with you."

"No!" Mateo held up his hands. "If you don't meet Topher on the court, he'll be outnumbered and will lose the game. And"—Mateo pursed his lips, his gaze darting to the window again—"you might lose your cred if that happens."

Aldo nodded. His brother was always looking out for him and his reputation. "Well, try to finish up quick so you can join us. Just scribble down some lines."

"Yeah, I'll do that." Mateo turned and hurried away.

Aldo didn't understand his brother's need to get a good grade in art. He didn't understand his brother's need to take an art class. He supposed it was for the easy A. But it seemed more trouble than it was worth if he was always doing extra credit.

Mateo had a reputation to protect outside. Turning on his heel, he started for the doors that would lead him to the courtyard when he collided with another person. His harsh tongue was all set to light into the guy who wasn't watching where he was going until he realized it was a girl.

Manners immediately engaged, he reached out to steady the soft form. He knew better than to grab too low or too high. With perfect, gentle-manly aim, he caught hold of a bony elbow. That's when a strand of red hair fell into his face.

The wisp of hair was like fire as it brushed his cheeks. That tendril of fire swiped at the corner of his mouth, blazing a trail across his lower lip. Aldo inhaled and smelled warm cinnamon. He didn't need to pull back to know that he was holding his nemesis in his arms. The sensation of falling down told him it was her.

Was this it? Had she won the game they'd been playing all these years? Was this moment his downfall?

"Get your hands off me, Aldo Matthews."

Elayne Jade had a heart-shaped mouth. Much like a mountain. Aldo loved watching it compress into twin peaks. It always did that when she said his name.

"You need to watch where you're going," she said. "You could hurt someone."

"You were the one looking down, not me."

"You could've moved around me."

Why would he do that? If he did, he wouldn't get to see her lips do that thing he liked. He wouldn't get to smell that hot cinnamon of Christmas that was on her skin year-round.

And then there was her hair. The color had lightened over the years. It was a softer shade of red. More like the carrots in his mother's garden.

"What are you staring at?" she demanded.

"Carrots."

"What?"

"Your hair looks like carrots."

Those carrots were sweet. Aldo always snacked on them when it was his chore to harvest. They were one of the only vegetables he didn't balk at eating when they were set before him on the dinner table.

"Ouch." Aldo rubbed at his chest where Elayne had slammed her algebra book.

"You are the meanest boy in the whole school. No, the whole town, Aldo Matthews."

And with that, she stormed off. But Aldo had gotten to see her lips make the M shape again. They remained pursed in the two peaks as she stormed off.

She left him standing on his own two feet. So this wasn't the scene of his downfall. The game was still on.

CHAPTER FOUR

Aldo Matthews smiled at her from the open bathroom door. That uptilt of his mouth scrambled Elayne's brains, and she had to look away. When her gaze dipped, she was confronted by something far worse: Aldo's bare torso.

He wore dark slacks that hugged his thick thighs so indecently that Elayne thought it might be best to call Social Services. The tails of a crisp white dress shirt hung open around the pants, like they were happy to enjoy the show. The curtain was open on the main stage, which was a six—no, make that an eight-pack of toned abdominal muscles. Who had an eight-pack?

Aldo Matthews did, that's who. Try as she

might, Elayne couldn't wrest her eyes away from the glistening, sculpted indecency of it all. Until she caught sight of that perpetual smirk on his face.

He always wore that expression. Like he knew he was God's gift to women. Physically, she couldn't argue with that notion. Aldo clearly broke the mold. The problem was always when he parted those lips and spoke that made the record scratch.

"There's my beautiful bride," he said. "How'd you sleep?"

Those words made no sense to Elayne. So she didn't address them. She addressed the far more pressing manner.

"What are you doing in my room?"

"My room," he said, chucking a thumb at his chest.

His still very bare chest. He'd lifted that thumb from the bottom of his shirt where he'd begun the slow task of slipping each button into its hole. He stopped to clarify the room's ownership. His hand now made the trek back to the shirttails to resume the job.

Elayne tore her gaze away and took another glance around the hotel room. That's when she noticed the bed was on the opposite side. The window had been reversed, too. And the television was in a different place. It was a mirror image of the room she had been staying in the last two nights.

"What am I doing in your room?" She asked the question out loud but more to herself. "And what is this ring doing on my finger?"

With her right hand, Elayne clutched the sheets to her cami-covered chest. She raised her left hand and stared at the gold band with a modest diamond at its center. It was beautifully made. Understated but still elegant. Like the jewel at the center had no need to boast. Like it knew its purpose: to show that it was a sign of devotion.

Aldo raised an eyebrow at her. "That's what happens when a man vows to love and cherish a woman for the rest of his days. He gives her a ring as a symbol."

Elayne opened her mouth. Then closed it. She opened it again because she needed air, but her brain had gone offline, so there was no mechanism to remind her how to breathe.

Had Aldo always been that big? Had his shoulders always been that broad? Had that cruel mouth always looked so ripe with the threat of pleasure?

He strode across the room. His shirt was

buttoned. Not all the way. There was still a peek-aboo of that broad chest with the last two buttons hanging open.

He reached for Elayne's left hand. It was still held out in front of her. He wrapped his large fingers around hers in a warm, firm grip. And wonder of wonders, Elayne let him. Because it felt…

Never mind what it felt like. It was wrong. It was all wrong.

"Vows?" she managed.

"Hmm," he hummed as he sat on the bed, bringing her hand to his mouth like a duke in a regency romance novel.

Elayne didn't snatch her hand back. She didn't have the energy to. Her head was spinning. From lack of oxygen? From the impossibility of this situation? From the hangover migraine? Though that last one was slowly ebbing away ever since he'd taken her hand.

Feeling exhausted, Elayne pressed her back against the headboard. Aldo leaned closer, as though he belonged in her personal space. The scent of minty soap and clean male assaulted her nose and made her brain scramble.

Aldo reached up his hand and tugged at one of

her curls. He'd never been this close to her. Heat radiated off him like he was a furnace. She suddenly felt too hot to keep the sheets around her. But she didn't dare let them drop. They were her only defense.

"The ring tells everyone else that you're off limits." He turned her hand over and pressed warm kisses into her palm.

"Is that what this is?" she asked.

"Is that what what is?"

Aldo rested his cheek in her palm and gazed at her. The stretch of his lips made her stupid. She'd watched him grin at other girls, and they had tittered. Elayne was on the verge of tittering. She snatched her hand back. This whole scenario was finally beginning to make sense.

"You tricked me into marrying you so that other guys would stay away from me?"

"Well, yeah, that is kind of the idea of holy matrimony."

Aldo leaned closer, aiming that grin at her. Was he about to kiss her? It was just too much. Even more because a part of her was curious as to what his lips would feel like against hers. What his mouth would taste like first thing in the morning… later in the evening…

But no. This was Aldo Matthews. Her mortal enemy. Her nemesis.

"I would never marry you." Her voice was hoarse. Likely because her statement lacked conviction.

Aldo blinked, a hard blink as though she'd slapped him in the face. He recovered quickly, though, and the smirk came back full force. "Your actions from last night would call you a liar."

He rubbed his thumb over the diamond on her left hand. Elayne shook her head. She snatched her hand away and slipped out of the bed. Then immediately grabbed for her shirt when she remembered she only wore a cami.

"This is a cruel joke, Aldo Matthews."

He was staring at her. At her lips. He always did that whenever she said his name. Like he detested the fact that she had to put his name in her mouth.

"I know you hate me but—" Elayne had to take a breath and turn from him when her lip trembled ever so slightly. "But I never thought..."

"I don't hate you. I never have."

His voice was soft. So soft that she was tempted to turn around. Aldo Matthews didn't do anything softly. But there was still a quiver in her lower lip.

"Of course you do," she said to the wall. "You've tormented me since the first day I met you."

His silence had Elayne peeking over her shoulder. There was no smirk on Aldo's face. He stared at her, dumbfounded.

"You've called me names. Raggedy Andy and carrot."

Again, the dumbfounded look remained as he sat on the bed. He looked at her like he had no idea what she was talking about. Like they'd had two different versions of their childhood.

"It was a game," he said finally. "It was all a part of the game we played."

"What game?" Elayne turned to face him fully. "The game where you hurt my feelings and laugh about it?"

"I... hurt your feelings?"

He stood, rising impossibly tall. But the way he looked down at her made Elayne feel small. She couldn't maintain eye contact with him. That mischievous hazel gaze looked off. Like, literally off. Like a light had gone out.

"I don't know what happened last night," she said, tugging her shirt over her head. "We both must have gotten drunk."

"You don't remember anything?"

"No." She bent down to pull on one and then the other shoe. "Do you?"

He didn't answer. He must have forgotten, too. But he was surprisingly steady for a guy waking up with a hangover.

"Luckily, we didn't take things too far," Elayne continued. "We can get this annulled, and it'll be like it never happened. No one needs to know."

More silence from the other side of the room. At least the smirk was gone. His lips were a thin line, as though he was chewing on the inside. It was the longest Elayne had known him to be silent.

Good, that had to mean he was finally seeing this conundrum for what it was.

"Aldo?" Elayne approached him carefully, tentatively. Like she would an unknown, injured dog on the street. The mutt might lick at the hand extended to it. Or the mongrel might lash out and take a bite out of her. It was a fifty-fifty chance with Aldo Matthews. "It's time we grew up and put this childish feud behind us. I don't want to fight with you anymore."

"I like fighting with you."

There was no bite behind his words. His expression was confused, as though Elayne was taking away his favorite chew toy. This man would never change. What had they put in that drink last night to make her consider for even a second that this was a good idea?

"I can't walk out of this room with you. It'll ruin my reputation as a counselor to impressionable kids."

Something shifted in his posture. A stiffness that she'd never seen before. Elayne realized she was looking at the disciplined soldier.

"Fine," he said. "I'll leave."

He strode forward to the door. Each step measured. His features were set in an unreadable mask. The sound of his shoes impacting the carpet was like the staccato of a drumbeat. When he reached for the door handle, Elayne stopped him with a last request.

"You won't tell anyone?"

He looked over his shoulder at her. The smirk was firmly back in place. A quizzical brow raised as he took her in. "Me and Elayne Jade? Who would believe me?"

The light in his eyes was still out, but there was vulnerability there. Elayne had the urge to smooth his brow. But she quickly shut that down. This was Aldo Matthews. Even though they'd just made a truce, he was the same bully from her childhood.

Breaking the gaze, Elayne reached down to pull the ring off her finger. It wouldn't budge.

"Keep it," he said, opening and closing the door behind him.

When he was gone, she felt the emptiness of the room all the way down to her toes. Her chest hurt, like her heart had slipped and fallen down on something hard. What had happened last night?

CHAPTER FIVE

"Hey bro, I forgot something at my locker." Mateo chucked a thumb over his shoulder as he twisted his upper body to move in the opposite direction without breaking his stride.

It was a move that caught more than many of the passes Aldo had thrown at him during their first year on the varsity football team. Seeing the move performed in the senior class hallway and not on the field had Aldo twisting his lips. That and the direction Mateo was headed.

"Bro, your locker is the other way," Aldo called after his twin's retreating form.

But Mateo was too busy dodging bodies as though he was indeed on the football field and headed to the end zone. He made a left turn that would lead him straight into the Creative Arts hallway where the theater, band, and art rooms were housed.

A crease formed on Aldo's brow, and he scratched his head at the empty hole his brother left in the crowd of upperclassmen. Mateo's behavior had been weirder and weirder as they approached their eighteenth birthday. It would soon be time to enlist, but his twin seemed to be dragging his feet.

"Hey, what's up, Al?"

Aldo didn't like his name being cut in half. Darius Cox, a third string tight end, often called his twin Matt. Aldo was proud of his Hispanic heritage. But he'd corrected Darius one too many times. The kid couldn't seem to learn—which was likely why he stayed on the bench all last season and it looked like he'd be keeping his spot warm this season as well. Aldo didn't want to waste his breath on the kid. Besides, he saw someone else he'd much rather talk to.

It had been over a week since he'd talked to Elayne Jade. She'd gone on a leadership summit Friday afternoon before the Homecoming game. He had no idea whose bright idea it was to have a conference during his big game. They'd won with Aldo launching the ball into his brother's hands twice and getting past a blitz himself that scored the winning touchdown.

It had been epic. They were still talking about it. Would be talking about that game for years to come. But Elayne hadn't seen a moment of it.

Someone had to have told her about it, though. The leadership conference had only been a few towns away. He wondered if she'd gasped as they described his fancy footwork around the defensive players who'd tried to take him down. Maybe her eyes had lit up when she learned how he ran thirty-three yards to score. If she had, he bet her forehead did that wrinkly thing when she was surprised.

The last time he'd seen her forehead wrinkle was when she'd worn a yellow headband. The yellow made her hair look an even brighter red than usual. The band had also pulled on her forehead, making her eyes look wide. It had reminded him of the great owl that stood in a tree in the woods bordering the Flying Cross and Silver Star ranches. The bird had the softest looking feathers that begged a boy to climb a tree and touch it. But the bird was fierce and proud.

Aldo had gotten pecked before he felt a single feather.

Unfortunately, when he'd made the comparison out loud, Elayne had snapped at him. Much like the owl. She'd called him a rat that deserved to be swept up by a winged predator, then stormed off.

She'd been doing that more and more lately in their epic battles. Instead of engaging him and trying to take him down like a nemesis should, she'd sigh, roll her eyes, and retreat. Each time she did, Aldo's chest would tighten, and any words would get locked in his throat.

"Here comes your sworn enemy."

The creases deepened beneath Aldo's brow. He wasn't sure where the voice had come from. He turned to see Darius standing shoulder to shoulder with him as though they were friends. They were not friends. And he needed to know that.

"Been running a little interference on that front for you, bro."

Aldo took a split second to try to figure out what Darius could possibly mean. But that fraction of a second was too long to waste on the kid. With a shake of his head, Aldo turned from Darius and took a step toward Elayne. It was her bright smile that stopped him in his tracks.

He'd seen her smile from afar plenty of times over the years. Just like the first time he'd seen her, it made something flutter in his belly. His heart was like a stone skipping across the water. He had to swallow a few times before he could get his lips to part to let air down his lungs.

"Her knees are still knotted, but I think I'm pretty close to working out that particular kink and then—"

Aldo loved action films. His favorite part of any action film was always the slow-motion stride. Especially if things slowed down to a hard rock anthem. Those were the best.

Things didn't happen like that in real life. They sped up. In one second, Darius was smirking at him. His lips were moving as his gaze slid past Aldo to leer at Elayne.

In the next second, Darius wasn't there. He was flat on the ground and there was blood seeping out of his cracked lip. It was an improvement as there were no longer foul words coming out of his mouth and his eyes were closed and not on Elayne.

Behind him, Aldo heard a feminine scream. He knew it was Elayne without turning around. That's when the slow motion started.

Time slowed as Aldo glanced over his shoulder

at the firebrand storming toward him. In that fraction of a second, Aldo knew that he would do anything—*anything*—to scoop Elayne up in his arms and protect her from anything and anyone who would make her scream in hurt, in fear, or in outrage.

The second thing he knew was that he was the cause of her outrage at this moment. Whatever game Darius was running on her, his smart, beautiful, no-nonsense girl had fallen for it. She'd fallen for Darius' game and not his. Well, that wasn't going to fly. She was his nemesis and no one else's.

As time continued its slow-motion action roll, Aldo leaned down to whisper into Darius' ear. It was only a few words. By the look on Darius' bruised face, Aldo knew the message was received loud and clear.

Then he was being wrenched off Darius by surprisingly strong hands. He backed off, helpless not to do anything Elayne commanded of him. The slap across his face stung but not more than the words she spat at him.

"Aldo Matthews, you are the worst," she said. "Absolutely rotten to the core. I knew it the first time I laid eyes on you, and you haven't changed an iota."

Aldo knew what an iota was. It was the ninth letter in the Greek alphabet. So it didn't mean exactly what she thought it meant. But his attention wasn't focused on her misuse of the word.

As always, Aldo was fixated on Elayne's mouth. The way it moved and formed words. But today, the words penetrated. His heart stilled from those skips. His belly clenched like it was empty.

"You can't date him," said Aldo.

"You cannot tell me who to date or not. You cannot believe that I would listen to anything you say."

"You don't know him."

"You don't know me. You don't know anything about me."

Aldo looked at her, dumbfounded. He knew everything about her. He knew she loved a good cup of tea, but she liked it weak. He watched her from across the cafeteria and saw her dunk the tea bag exactly three times before taking it out of her cup and sitting it aside.

He knew that her favorite pens were the Paper Mate Ink Joys. She preferred to write with the purple one when she was making any corrections instead of the red. She hadn't said it out loud, but he guessed it was to do with her hair color. Whenever she opened a package of new pens, she always left the red ones in the library. Aldo had a collection in his sock drawer at home.

A drop of red blood smeared on her thumb as she cradled Darius' face. The kid winced at her touch. He outright recoiled when he caught sight of Aldo's murderous glare.

Proving he wasn't as dumb as he looked, Darius shook Elayne's help off. He crab-walked backwards until he was on his feet. Then he took off down the hall without so much as a word to her.

Elayne watched him go, her wide eyes slowly casting downward to the linoleum floor of the senior class hallway. She looked devastated at the rejection. She turned that anger on Aldo.

"From now on, don't look my way. Go in the other direction if you see me. I don't want to see your face. I don't want to hear your voice. I don't want anything to do with you ever, Aldo Matthews."

CHAPTER SIX

Elayne slammed the hotel room door behind her. She walked away with quick steps, terrified Aldo was lurking behind some corner. She needn't have worried. The hall remained silent.

When she found her room, she double-checked the number before sliding the keycard out of her skirt pocket and opening the door. Once inside, she leaned back against the frame. She barely made it to the bed before her body sagged.

What in the heck had just happened?

Flicking on the bedside lamp, the low light provided no answers. The ring on her finger shimmered at her as though beckoning her to lean forward so that it could tell her its secrets.

Elayne didn't fall for it. She didn't want to know any secrets from this ring. She wanted it off her finger. But another few tugs and the piece of jewelry refused to budge.

She glared at it. Then she gave in. Raising her left hand, she leaned her ear to the ring. And… nothing. Flopping down on the bed, Elayne covered her face with her hands and moaned.

Married? To her worst enemy? This could not be happening to her.

Needing to take something off, Elayne stripped out of her clothes. Padding to the bathroom on bare feet, she hopped in the shower. At first, she let the cold water run. She needed the shock to her system. Unfortunately, the cold didn't wash away her reality. The diamond continued to sparkle at her under the chilly sprinkles.

Turning the dial over to the red markings for hot, Elayne waited for the temperature to rise. It took a good three minutes, which served her right. In those three minutes, she swore that she would never drink again—going so far as to consider giving up chocolate.

By the time the hot water came out of the shower head, Elayne decided there was no need to be that harsh. She was going to need some cocoa courage to deal with the fact that she was now Mrs. Aldo Matthews.

The thought sent a shiver through her. Though unlike when she was a young girl thinking about Aldo, that shiver wasn't cold. It didn't make her belly grumble in disgust. Not with the vision of those eight-pack abs etched forever on her brain.

And then there was that kiss he'd laid on her knuckles, in the center of her palm. Her hand still felt hot from where he'd laid his mouth. It felt like the impression might still be there.

Elayne pressed her lips to the center of her palm. All she tasted was cool water.

Giving herself a shake, she scrubbed at her flesh and washed her hair to get all memories and any evidence of him off her. When she climbed out of the stall and patted herself dry, she could still smell him on her.

Despite the hot water and soap, that scent of strong male lingered. Where had he touched her? Probably all over her back if he'd been lying beside her all night. Had they… cuddled?

The thought should have twisted her gut. In a way, it did. But the writhing was warm and pleasurable, like being bundled up in a thick, heavy blanket set before a cozy fire.

And that was enough of that!

Elayne pulled on clean clothes. Then she doused herself in perfume, spritzing her wrists and the air around her a couple times more than was decent. But she had no plans to be sniffed by anyone. She still had one more session of the conference to go to before she was out of here. She would just sit in the back of the room, like the older and married attendees wanted her to, and for once, she wouldn't complain about it.

Peering out into the hall, she looked left and right. But she didn't see him. Was she expecting to see him?

Yeah, she was. Elayne was expecting—hoping—Aldo would jump out of from a hiding space with a camera crew in tow and shout *Psych!* Or maybe he'd hit her over the head with something and she'd wake up from this nightmare.

But the halls were empty, and her eyes were wide open. The headache had dulled at least. If she got a cup of tea in her with some toast, she just might be able to fake normal.

The elevator ride down, which was just three floors, let her know normal was not in the cards for her today. The fluorescent lights in the main lobby made her doubt normal would be available tomorrow, either. Rubbing at her temple and squinting, the bar area came into view, and so did a few flashes from her time there last night.

The amber liquid in a crystal glass. A male's face getting in her space. But that wasn't Aldo's. Had someone hit on her?

She could remember seeing Aldo appear in the mirror, his face stony as he glared at the guy. What was the guy's name?

Elayne couldn't remember the guy's name. She wasn't sure if she'd learned it. He was there and gone so quickly. And then there was just Aldo.

Aldo had smiled, and it had dazzled her. Even in her memory, his smile stopped her in her tracks. Elayne stood staring at the barstool where they'd sat and… talked.

They'd talked for a long time. But for the life of her, she couldn't remember a single thing that had been said. She also couldn't remember how they'd gone from the bar to the City Hall for a marriage license and holy matrimony.

A chorus of laughter came from a private dining area off to the side of the bar. Elayne recognized the first couple that came out of the room. With the doors slowly closing, she recognized even more of her colleagues seated at tables in pairs.

More memories from last night started coming back to her, though this time, they had nothing to do with a broad-chested soldier. The face that came to Elayne's mind was a woman's.

Elayne had been speaking to Shirley Moss after dinner. She'd tried to corner the head counselor for the county after the meal about incorporating more mindfulness techniques in the curriculum. Dr. Moss had only given Elayne a perfunctory smile as she'd looked over her shoulder at the couples gathering at the exit. With a promise to discuss it later, she'd extracted herself from the lone single woman at the conference and made her way out the door with the other married couples.

She wondered what had been decided in that breakfast meeting that she hadn't been a part of. That she hadn't been invited to because she didn't have a ring on her finger.

Elayne glanced down at the ring on her finger. She'd forgotten it was there. She tugged at it. It still wouldn't come off. Maybe Aldo had put super glue on it? Maybe that was the joke.

"Ms. Jade? Is that...? Are you...?"

Dr. Moss' gaze and index finger were pointed at Elayne's hand. Like a kid with their hand in a cookie jar, Elayne's first instinct was to put it behind her back. She was too slow, and Dr. Moss grabbed at it, holding it high.

"Oh, my dear, why didn't you tell us? When did this happen? You have to come into breakfast and tell us all about it."

"It?"

"Your engagement." Dr. Moss let out a delighted giggle.

Her engagement? Of course, Dr. Moss would think she was engaged because she had been ringless less than twenty-four hours ago. What irresponsible guider and counselor of children would be fool enough to elope in the middle of the night?

"But..." Elayne searched her addled brain desperately for a solution, or at least a stalling tactic. "But there's the last session."

Dr. Moss waved the notion away. "We're not missing anything. Besides, we can talk about curriculum at the luncheon before we depart."

There was a luncheon? Elayne hadn't seen that on the schedule of events.

"That's where the real movers and shakers on the curriculum committee will be. But first, we need to discuss that darling ring and your new fiancé."

CHAPTER SEVEN

"You're just the kind of soldier we could use in an operation like Manned Power, son."

Aldo's right eye twitched. He'd learned not to go on wincing when a superior called him *son* during Basic Training. It still rankled him. The word rang like a gong between his ears. There were only two men who had earned the right to call him that.

It was just another factor that soured his notion of joining the military contractor outfit. Manned Power specialized in providing escort and protection for high-risk figures. The notion caused Aldo's left eye to twitch. He'd spent his entire career in service to everyday people who oftentimes couldn't fend for themselves. Not those who'd become wealthy putting others' lives in danger.

Still, Aldo pocketed the card before heading out of the conference room. The day had pretty much been a bust. He hadn't vibed with a single contractor outfit at the event. Vibing was important to Aldo. He hadn't liked all the men and women he'd served with. But he had respected each and every one of them.

The glossy sales pitches and obvious lies from the suits at the conference left Aldo feeling cold. He knew there were reputable military contracting outfits. None of them had shown up this week.

Maybe he'd just reenlist. But the thought of serving without his twin—without any of his brothers—didn't warm him. All of the Matthews brothers were at home now, all married or soon to be. Except for him and Mateo. Maybe he could join his brother on his new JROTC venture.

"Matthews? Aldo Matthews, is that you, son?"

Aldo winced. Not at being called *son*. It was because of who had called him that. "Officer Moss, how are you, sir?"

Moss had gotten to know Aldo well as a foster kid. He'd been more than rough around the edges, having just lost his parents and having English as a second language. He'd lashed out on more than one occasion. Officer Moss had had the dubious job of reining him in.

"It's Captain now." Captain Moss grasped Aldo's hand for a firm shake. There might be gray at his temples, but the man was still as strong as an ox. "Look at how you filled out. And a soldier too, if I heard right."

"Yes, sir, a pilot."

"Well, I'll be. I always knew you'd make something of yourself if you just kept your nose clean."

Aldo sniffed at that.

"You looking for contract work?" Moss asked, glancing over Aldo's shoulder at the hiring convention banners.

Moss didn't wait for Aldo to answer. He pulled a card out of his wallet and handed it to him. It was on cheap card stock, but it proudly proclaimed the officer's rank and name.

"We need help on the force, if you're interested in staying in your hometown."

"Me? On the police force?" Aldo would've laughed if not for the serious expression on Moss' face.

"You never were a criminal mastermind, but

you always had that mischievous streak in you. I need a man who thinks like you on my side. Help keep our town and its residents safe. Think about it?"

With a nod and firm clap on his shoulder, Moss took off, leaving Aldo thinking about it. Every thought that flitted through his head, he liked. He liked the notion of staying home and being close to his family. He liked the idea that he could protect the place and the people whose faces he knew.

Each thought left a pleasant sensation, leaving a sweet taste in his mouth. Either this was the best idea he'd ever had, or it was his twinsense activated. Still holding the card in his left hand, Aldo reached his other hand into his pocket and dialed his brother.

"Hello."

"Hey, bro."

"Were you eating or drinking something sweet right now? I swear I just got a sugar rush. Oh wait, it was Miguel's party last night. He made cake?"

"Yeah," Mateo confirmed. "Yeah, we all had cake."

"You better have saved me some. From our bond, I can taste it was really sweet. Mmmm."

There was silence on the other end of the line.

The sweet taste in Aldo's mouth soured. Was his brother that loath to share their new foster nephew's cake?

"These meetings are going great. I think you'd be interested in a couple of these contracts."

There was one contractor who had been hired to help build a school in a third-world country. That kind of job was right up Mateo's alley. If Mateo gave an inkling that he'd take that kind of job, Aldo would go along. Looking down at the card in his hand, Aldo decided not to give him any of those details.

Not that Mateo would listen. He was still talking. Going on and on about the JROTC program, which essentially was Mateo building a school on their home turf. The idea wasn't looking so bad to Aldo anymore. Especially if he made the police force and could stop by and hang with his brother.

Staying in town had its other benefits. It wasn't just his family he could see on a regular basis. There were other people Aldo wouldn't mind catching sight of. Like a particular redheaded woman who Aldo had never been able to get out of his mind. She was so much in his mind that he swore he saw her seated at the bar.

"Listen, Aldo, you should know I'm dating—"

"Andy!"

Aldo's feet were moving before he was conscious of making the command. The closer he got to the woman, the more he knew he was right. It was her.

"Elayne?" asked Mateo in his ear. "What are you doing with Elayne Jade?"

"She's here. She's at the conference hall."

"Just stay away from her."

"How can I stay away from her when she's coming right at me?"

"Look, Aldo, just—"

"Gotta go, bro. Save me some cake."

And with that, he cut his connection with his twin. But once he got within two strides of the bar, he came to a dead stop. Aldo's last interaction with this woman hadn't been the best. Their siblings had to separate them and send them to opposite ends of a parking lot.

Aldo had stewed, sitting in his car while not being able to catch another sight of Elayne. He'd glared at his brother and her red-haired sister. Again, he wondered how people insisted they looked alike when the differences were so clear to him.

Kailyn's red hair was at least two shades lighter

than Elayne's. Kailyn's face was round where Elayne's was clearly heart-shaped. And there was something too quiet and meek about Kailyn where Elayne was nothing but fire.

"What can I get you, son?" asked the bartender.

The man couldn't have had more than a couple of years on Aldo. Was Aldo just inspiring men who wanted to be father figures to speak to him today? Before he could wince, Elayne did it for him. She tossed back a brown liquid that looked thicker than whisky and her facial features scrunched in on themselves.

It was the most adorable thing Aldo had ever seen in his life. The two strides of distance were a thing of the past, and he was standing in front of her.

"Excuse me," came a gruff voice behind him.

Aldo hadn't even realized there was another person sitting with her. It didn't matter who he was. With a menacing look tossed over his shoulder, the man squeaked off the bar and scurried out of sight, leaving Aldo alone with Elayne.

She opened her eyes from the wince and blinked at him. Then she blinked a few more times. "Am I having a nightmare?"

Aldo watched her lips move. They rounded to

make the vowel sounds and compressed on the consonants. He took a step closer, unable to help himself. That rumble in his belly he'd always felt as a kid at the sight of her, that skip of his heartbeat. He knew what those meant now.

"Must be a nightmare because this day can't get any worse."

He wanted to reach out to her brow and smooth the creases there. He wanted to take her chin in his hand and tilt her head high where it should be. He wanted to kiss that mouth. Dear God did he want that kiss.

But he couldn't do any of those things. Not yet. Maybe he could if he put a hurting on whoever made her unhappy.

"Tell me about it," he coaxed.

Maybe it was the chocolate glop of alcohol that loosened her tongue. Because she did. She told him. Elayne Jade confided in Aldo Matthews.

"I'm getting shut out at work because I don't have a ring on my finger. Can you believe that? A piece of jewelry is stopping me from getting any promotions or more responsibilities that could lead to career advancement."

"I have a ring."

Mateo had their mother's prized Raggedy Ann

and Andy dolls, but Aldo had inherited her ring. He pulled it out from the necklace he wore around his neck. The one that also held his dog tags.

Sliding it off the chain and presenting it to Elayne felt right. Like when he officially became a Matthews. Like when he received his wings. That's what it felt like to hold the modest diamond out to this woman.

"Will this solve your problem?" he asked.

Elayne stared at the offering, unfocused. She was drunk, meaning she could not consent. So that kiss would have to wait.

"Why would you give me a ring? You hate me."

"I've never hated you."

"You call me names. You call me Raggedy Andy."

Aldo recognized the woman was drunk, but he knew for a fact that he wasn't a saint. And so he did it. He reached up and grabbed a strand of that vibrant red hair that was so like his mother's prized dolls. He ran his finger through it the way he'd always wanted to.

"We're always fighting," Elayne continued, completely oblivious to his rapture in her hair.

"Yeah," Aldo agreed. "It's the only way you'll talk

to me. You decided you didn't like me. But I like you, Elayne Jade."

"You like me?"

There went that crease between her brows. Reluctant to loosen his hold of her hair, Aldo used his free hand to smooth the furrows in her forehead. Her skin was the softest texture he'd ever touched.

"You're the smartest girl I know."

"You think I'm smart?"

"And beautiful."

Elayne reared back, but she didn't get far. Aldo cupped her cheeks in both hands. Her green gaze went wide. "I think I'm drunk."

"I think so too."

"Or maybe I'm drugged." Her eyes dipped to his lips and then back to his eyes and then flitted away to the bar where her drink sat empty. "Did you slip something into my drink?"

"I would never do anything to hurt you, Elayne. Let me prove it. Take my ring."

"Are you asking me to marry you?" she said.

"Yes."

"You think I'll say yes?"

"No. Not yet. But maybe one day. Until that day, I'm going to prove I'm the one for you."

CHAPTER EIGHT

"Oh, I can totally believe every word you just said. Aldo Matthews is a conniving, lying trickster, and I can't wait for him to leave this town and leave us in peace."

In fairness, Kailyn hadn't said any of those things to Elayne. But she hadn't needed to. These were the facts about the man she loathed. The man she was now married to. The gold band burned her hip inside her pocket.

Elayne had finally gotten the wedding ring off her finger after much soap and oil and prayer. She paced the length of the living room floor, getting herself worked up all over again. The impact of her heels striking the floor brought to mind a booted army storming the capitol. Her rigid shoulders were like a general preparing to give the final order to decimate the opposition. Her curled lip looked like a devil who would enjoy glaring down at all the carnage he'd been a party in creating.

"That family is nothing but a bunch of brutes," Elayne went on. She punched her fist in the air and pointed her finger to punctuate her statement. It was a pretty brief statement, but her hand gestures continued long after she'd stopped talking. She did not stop pacing.

"I don't think you're being fair," said Kailyn. "The Matthews are decent people as a whole. There's only really one bad apple in that bunch."

Elayne came to an abrupt halt in her pacing and rounded on Kailyn. "I thought you said Mateo threw the first punch."

While Elayne had been gone and getting tricked into marrying one Matthews twin, the other had begun seducing her sister. Mateo Matthews had taken Kailyn out on a couple of dates and likely would've pulled the same marriage stunt if Elayne hadn't come back home early. The two Matthews twins were clearly up to something.

But what? What could marrying her and her sister be all about? When Elayne turned her attention back to her sister, she saw her recoil. Was it at the memory of the fight between brothers? The notion of Mateo and Aldo coming to blows made even less sense than this sham of a marriage. If the twin brothers were working in cahoots, why trade blows?

"Only because Aldo insulted me," Kailyn was saying.

One by one, Elayne curled her fingers into her palm until they were a tight fist. "I just wish I could have been there to see him go down. No—no, I wish I could've been the one to punch him in that proud nose of his. He thinks he's so handsome."

Elayne had stopped her forward march. Now she stood with her legs braced. The pounding continued as she punched her closed fist into her open palm. Her gaze went wistful, as though she was picturing that proud nose on that handsome face as she continued to punch into the center of her hand.

"Wait a minute." Elayne's attention came back to Kailyn. "What were you doing behind enemy lines in the first place?"

"They're not our enemy."

"Oh, you naïve girl. He's finally gotten to you, hasn't he?"

"What? Who?"

"Don't play dumb, Kailyn. I've seen the way Mateo Matthews used to look at you when we were kids. He was all puppy dog eyes while his brother was a pit bull."

Elayne knew her sister did not condone violence. But they were under attack. Why couldn't she see that? Likely because Elayne had Aldo's ring hidden in her pocket and she hadn't told her twin about the marriage.

"They're playing some kind of game with us," said Elayne.

"Who?"

Elayne threw back her head and let out an annoyed huff. "The Matthews twins."

"Mateo isn't playing with me. He has feelings for me. He said he has for a long time."

For a moment, Elayne simply stared at her sister. When Elayne finally spoke, her voice was a snarl. "Aldo said the same thing to me."

"Aldo? You had a conversation with Aldo?"

Elayne turned away from Kailyn and began to pace again. She wasn't ready to share her news with her sister. She wanted to solve the problem before she spoke of it with anyone.

Aldo Matthews had humiliated her one too many times. With her first high school boyfriend, who'd dumped her over text message after that nasty brawl in the hallway. All those times he called her that awful nickname Raggedy Andy.

"Elayne?"

"I hate him." Elayne flounced down into a chair and turned away, but not before she dabbed at her eyes. "I just hate him so much. I wish the earth would just open up and swallow him whole. But then it probably would spit him back out because the man is so distasteful."

Elayne's last words were barely intelligible because they were said on the tail end of a sob. That sob became a hiccup. Once the hiccup cleared, Elayne began to cry in earnest.

Kailyn rushed over to her twin to wrap her arms around the shaking form. She tried to squeeze her sister tightly and take on some of the burden. Elayne couldn't tell her that it wouldn't work this time. This was a burden her sister couldn't share with her.

"He tricked me, Kailyn."

"Who tricked you? Aldo?"

Elayne sniffled as she nodded her head. "And I fell for it."

"What did you fall for? What did he do?"

"Aldo Matthews tricked me into marrying him."

The weight Kailyn had been trying to take from Elayne forced Kailyn back on her haunches. When Elayne's vision unblurred and became clear, she saw her sister staring at her with wide, disbelieving eyes.

"I told him I wanted to annul it immediately." Elayne shrugged off Kailyn's touch and straightened her shoulders. "He said no. He thinks he's got me cornered for..." Elayne swiped angrily at the tears falling down her cheeks. "For whatever game he's trying to play. But I'm going to make his life miserable until he does give me that annulment and ends this sham of a marriage."

On Monday morning, she would get this taken care of. Then she would never have to see or think of Aldo Matthews again.

CHAPTER NINE

On Monday morning, Aldo got up and dressed in his uniform. He looked in the mirror and saw a carbon copy of himself. Though it wasn't an exact replica. For the first time, he started to notice how different he and his brother were.

There were worry lines at Aldo's eyes where Mateo's looked upbeat and happy. There was a sag to Aldo's shoulders where Mateo's were straight, ready to take on the world.

Aldo felt tired. He looked tired.

Mateo looked energized and happy. The man was in love. And the woman he loved returned his feelings. That much was evident in how Kailyn Matthews threw herself into Mateo's arms after she won the bid for the after-school program the two of them had been vying for for the past few days that Aldo had been out of town.

True, Mateo had eliminated any competition for her, including himself, so that the bid would be hers. When Aldo had tried to eliminate any competition between him and Elayne, he'd gotten an earful. That's where the wariness came in. But still, he couldn't stop himself from going into the fire that was Elayne Jade.

Most people had favorite colors. His birth mother's favorite color had been red on account of a doll. His adoptive mother's favorite had been mahogany, which was reddish brown.

For years, Aldo had thought Tessa Matthews loved that color because of a film starring her favorite actress, which she'd watched at least once a month on the old television in the family room. At her funeral, he'd learned that his second mother had fallen in love with the color after her husband planted a hibiscus shrub as a border around her garden.

The bush still thrived there today. Its reddish-brown foliage had never held Aldo's attention like it did for his twin brother. Whenever Mateo encountered anything with red, he usually treated it like a stoplight and came to a halt and stared at it with a stupid grin on his face.

Aldo didn't have a favorite color. But he did have a favorite letter. It was the letter M. The beginning of his new last name, which had given him a fresh start in life.

He liked the curves that made up the top of the letter. The symmetry of the form was pleasing to his eyes. Maybe another reason Aldo liked the shape of the M was because there were two curves in the letter—twin peaks.

Just as he reached the summit of one side, he would arrive in a valley and look up to see another mountain to climb. Though sometimes the twin mountains would flatten out, compressing into a thin line. He didn't like it when that happened.

Other times, the mountains would smoosh together, making the distance between them closer and the valley non-existent. In his mind, he thought of stretching his body out across the twin peaks. Maybe even tasting both summits at the same time.

"Are you even listening to me?"

Aldo blinked. He jerked his attention up. Way up past the purse of her top lip. Up beyond the flare of her nostrils. Higher to the blaze of those bright green eyes.

There, he had to pause. It always took him at least two seconds before he could orient himself in her gaze. Having Elayne Jade's full attention on him always made Aldo feel hot under his collar. The steam from that heat would fog up his brain.

He had to be careful because in those few moments, she could get the better of him. And if she got the better of him, he would be the one to lose in the game they had played since they were children. The game of who could make the other pop their top.

Aldo was the reigning champion of the game. With just a few well-placed words, he could rile Elayne up enough that those perfectly shaped lips would part, forming the most exquisite M shape he could ever imagine.

"I don't know what game you're playing at, Aldo Matthews, but I'm going to make you regret it."

Aldo had come to Kailyn's presentation with his brother. It wasn't so much that he wanted to support his brother's new girlfriend as he wanted to catch sight of his brother's girlfriend's sister. As soon as the meeting was over, Elayne stormed up to him, that red hair blazing a trail of fire, those green eyes igniting.

Her lips parted slightly. But the shape was all wrong. The right side of her mouth lifted higher than the left side, making the shape off-balance. He needed to find the right words to irritate her enough to get them back in alignment.

"You think I could regret anything more than finding myself hitched to you?" He hurled the words at her. And bingo! Her lips parted, but only briefly, before she huffed out an angry breath that made them bow a bit.

"Well, there's an easy fix to that."

Aldo felt something thump against his chest. At first, he didn't react to it. His heart often beat rapidly around Elayne Jade. It was the thrill of the game they played, and he knew he was winning.

"Just sign the annulment papers."

Her mouth compressed into a flat line as she breathed through her nose. Uh-oh. He was losing. The mountains were disappearing in the horizon of her face.

Victory had been so close. Where had he gone wrong?

Aldo looked down at the papers she had thrust

at him. In bold black letters, he saw words across the top. One word stood out to him.

Annulment.

Aldo recoiled at the word as though it were a snake weaving through his tranquil valley. That word had no place here. It did not belong between them.

"Well? What are you waiting for?" Elayne was saying. "You want to be rid of me, don't you? Sign the papers."

She flung the pages at him, but Aldo refused to catch them. Why would he? This was not what he wanted. This was not how he wanted to play the game. He had been so close to winning. Now it felt like he was not just losing this match, it felt like he might never win with her again.

The pages slipped free and cascaded down to the floor with abandon. Aldo saw why. The paperclip that had held them came loose and was now caught in Elayne's hair.

Without thinking, he reached up to snag the metallic clip. When he did so, his fingertips brushed against Elayne's cheek. Her lips parted on a sharp inhale. His gaze was immediately drawn to her mouth, where he saw it—two perfect twin peaks.

Climbing was the last thing on his mind. Conquering was what he wanted to do. Aldo wanted to take that perfectly shaped M and capture it in his mouth. He wanted to plunge into the valley between her top lip to find the treasure buried there. For the first time, he realized that was the prize in this game that they played.

If he won, which he had every intention of doing, then he could kiss Elayne Jade's perfect mouth.

A sound from across the hall jerked her attention away from him. Elayne blew out a long, low breath that she must have been holding. The exhalation compressed her lips, flattening the mountain Aldo had been about to conquer.

She pulled away from his hold before he could close his hands around her nape. The papers swished and crumpled under her feet as she stormed off. His first instinct was to give chase, but there was no need. He already had her cornered. He just needed to bide his time before he came out the inevitable victor.

He had no intentions of signing those annulment papers. Because they weren't married. At least not yet.

CHAPTER TEN

Elayne stormed into the front doors of the high school on the next morning after the school board meeting. She was dressed in full body armor. Boots with a thick stem that a military general would lift an appreciative brow at. A killer skirt that hugged her curves and ended just above the knee so that she had the mobility to kick down any door—or six-foot aviator.

Hmmm? That's what this outfit was missing: a pair of Aviator sunglasses would complete the look. But then no one would see the take-no-prisoners glare she wore. They also wouldn't see the bags under her eyes from the sleepless night.

Nightmares had plagued her dreams. Most of the visions behind her eyelids featured a dark-haired man grinning down at her. That grin was carnivorous. Like a shark. A shark licking its chops as it balled and unballed its fists. Or were those fins?

The shark's toothsome smirk came closer and closer. Elayne couldn't tell if he was going to kiss her silly or take a bite out of her. Worse than that, she didn't know which she wanted.

It didn't help that when she pulled open her front door this morning, she saw his face. Though it wasn't *his* face. It was his twin brother's face.

Mateo recognized her instantly in that way twins could always tell other twins apart. "Good morning, Elayne."

His warm smile took some of the fight out of her. But not all of it. She neither wanted to kiss Mateo nor carve him up. Unlike his obnoxious brother, Mateo was a decent human being. But he still shared a face with the enemy.

"Morning." She rushed past him. "I'm gonna be late. Don't make her late."

Elayne chucked her thumb at her sister, whose grin was so bright that Elayne once again wished she had that pair of Aviators. The heat bouncing off Kailyn and being absorbed by Mateo's adoring grin was enough to power a plane from here to

Europe. It was making Elayne a little green—and not the sick kind of green. Envy poured from her veins.

"Wouldn't dream of it," Mateo was saying, though how he formed words through that grin was a mystery. "I just brought her a treat for her first day on her after-school job."

Sweet. Mateo Matthews was sweet. Why couldn't he have rubbed off on his bitter brother? Probably because Aldo had shouldered his way out of their mother's womb, leaving Mateo to nurse his wounds.

That's why probably why Mateo's features were often scrunched in a wince when he stood in a crowd. His mouth often twisted before he stood up to speak in class. His smile back then had always been a bit self-deprecating, as though he was apologizing before he opened his mouth. She'd watched him do that a lot in their youth. He'd often get blamed for his brother's antics.

Elayne decided right then and there that she wouldn't do that to him any longer. Mateo made her sister happier than she'd ever seen Kailyn. It wasn't his fault that he was attached to that foul beast of a brother.

Too bad Mateo couldn't extricate himself fully

from Aldo. That was a feat Elayne had every intention of accomplishing for herself. She had been tipsy on that ill-fated night of their marriage.

Okay, she had been drunk. But she suspected Aldo hadn't been. So he'd done whatever it was that they'd done with a completely sober head.

What was he up to? What was his long game? She'd offered him a way out yesterday with those annulment papers. Why hadn't he taken them? And why had he stared at her mouth for so long, like he wanted to kiss her?

Or maybe take that bite out of her?

"You okay, Elayne?"

Mateo's voice was so like Aldo's that she jumped. If it hadn't been a half an octave deeper, she might've put that stem of her boot to good use. But she didn't want to start the workday by drop-kicking her sister's new boyfriend. So she did an about face and made for her car.

"I gotta get to work," she said, moving farther away from the happy couple's glow.

"Have a good day," Mateo called after her. "And Elayne..."

Elayne halted her forward march. She was hesitant to do an about face. Only because she didn't want to look into Mateo's happy face. She also didn't want to go back on her word of all of a minute ago to treat him separately from his brother. She allowed her upper body to perform a corner turn but kept her boots pointed in the direction of her car.

"Let me know if you need anything." Mateo stood with an arm at Kailyn's back. His words were heavy, pregnant with the twin that stood between him and Elayne.

Elayne nodded, chewing at the inside of her cheek. She was ready for a truce with Mateo. She was unsure if she was ready to have a Matthews as an ally.

But there one was. Standing in her doorway. A protective arm around her sister. An open and friendly smile extended her way. A bit of their warm front melted the edges of the cold around her.

"There you are," came a new voice, followed by a blast of cold. "Still shining brightly at being a newly engaged woman."

Mrs. Moss beamed at Elayne from the head counselor's office doorway. Her bright smile fell along with her gaze. When Elayne realized the woman was looking at her left hand—her bare left hand—she shoved her arm behind her back.

"Did something happen between you and your man?"

Elayne pressed her hand to her pocket where the ring was safely stored. She could have left it on her dresser this morning, but for some reason she was loath to leave it out of her sight. She pulled it from her pocket now. She presented the ring to Mrs. Moss and prepared to come clean.

"Oh, good," Mrs. Moss breathed a sigh of relief. "For a moment, I thought I was about to make a mistake."

"What mistake?"

"There's a spot open on the counseling curriculum committee. I put your name in the hat."

"You did?" Elayne's voice was breathless. This was the promotion she'd wanted for the last two years, but she'd been passed over.

"The only thing holding the committee back before was our uncertainty that you would stay put. So many single people move around and change jobs these days."

But that wasn't Elayne. This was the only home she'd ever known. The year she and her sister had spent as foster kids was long enough to let her know that she never wanted to be uprooted again. She had no plans to ever leave Honor Valley.

"Now that we know you're getting married and you'll put down roots and be settled, we think that you're the perfect person for the job."

Elayne opened her mouth to argue, to rage at the unfairness of each and every one of those statements, but her thoughts went blank. No, not blank. They swirled around in her head so fast and chaotically that she couldn't catch hold on to any of them.

"Your young man is Aldo Matthews, isn't that right? My husband saw the two of you together at the hotel bar. I suppose that was the night he proposed."

The sound of his name settled the whirlwind in Elayne's head. But she kept her mouth shut. She had never been a good liar. Mrs. Moss and her husband thought she and Aldo were engaged. They didn't know that truth, that she'd gotten married while drunk and couldn't even remember saying her vows.

She would have to set her straight soon. Especially since Aldo would be deploying again at some point in the near future.

"My husband's the police chief, you know. He said your man was applying to be on the force."

CHAPTER ELEVEN

Aldo reached over the desk and clasped the callused hand of his new boss. It was the first time he'd shaken the man's hand. In his youth, he'd been given many a stern talking to by the town's police chief. Today, the two faced each other, not quite as equals, but with equal respect.

"You'll make a great addition to the force," said Chief Moss. "Not only with your military training and instincts but also with your history in this town."

"My history, sir?" Aldo stood erect, years of training showing him how to react in front of his superiors. Though in his youth, he hadn't looked at Officer Moss as his superior. He'd regarded the man as another adult who thought he knew best how Aldo should live his life. The joke was on Aldo, because Moss had been right.

Before his adoption, Moss had warned Aldo to straighten up if he wanted to make something of himself. He'd urged Aldo to follow the rules instead of break them. He'd challenged Aldo with making friends instead of enemies.

"You were a troublemaker in this town," Moss said now.

Aldo held his breath to hold in the retort that wanted to come out. That part of his personality hadn't been trained out of him quite so thoroughly. It would forever need reinforcements.

"I half expected you to be behind bars, not handing you a pair of handcuffs."

"Times have changed, and I grew up."

"That you have, son." Chief Moss nodded approvingly at Aldo, lessening the unpleasant sting of that last word. "You're still young enough to be in the service. Still a few medals to earn. Why leave now?"

A red-haired fire sprang into Aldo's vision. Green eyes that made him feel grounded stared back at him through his mind's eye. And then there were those lips, the only mountain Aldo wanted to summit, or get lost in, or even fall from. He couldn't imagine leaving the place where she made her home.

"I was thinking about contract work," is what he said to Chief Moss. It was the whole reason he'd gone to the Purple Heart Ranch that past weekend. But Aldo had found something else entirely that he wanted to dedicate his life to. "Now I want to settle down, start a family."

Chief Moss nodded again. The twinkle in his eye made Aldo think of his biological father, whose hazel gaze was often filled with laughter and pride as he looked down on his twin sons. Father Matthews had the same look of delight and honor when he looked at Aldo.

"I also want to be a part of the community I fought so hard for," Aldo continued. "Not just for the citizens of my country, but for the people in this very town. The residents of Honor Valley gave me a lot of second chances. I want to show them that I've earned them."

A broad smile spread across Moss's face. "When can you start your training?"

"As soon as you're ready for me."

"We'll start tomorrow."

Aldo left the chief's office and the police precinct with a pep in his step. Mission Win

Himself a Wife was in full effect. He'd secured gainful employment. Now he just needed to locate his woman.

As though he'd conjured her out of the blue, Elayne Jade walked toward him on the street. More like stormed toward him. She was dressed to stop a man's heart in a skirt that embraced each and every one of her curves. The boots on her feet tapped out a battle cry. Aldo prepared for a complete surrender.

When she stood toe to toe with him, Aldo's instincts were to reach for her. To pull her close and kiss her silly. The expression on her face, that perfect-shaped M, told him that a smooch would not be welcome.

Her expression had been fierce. The corner of her mouth quavered when she tilted her head back and stared into his eyes. Her features didn't soften. She might have laid down one of the weapons she had brought to this battle against him.

"What are you doing?" she demanded.

Aldo's gaze tracked the movement of her mouth, trying to hold himself back from claiming what he swore would soon be his. "Deciding whether or not it's safe to kiss you right now."

Every weapon she'd loaded fell out of her hold.

She swallowed hard, making a choked sound. It was all he needed. Her defenses were down, and he was a trained warrior.

He reached for her, wrapping both arms around her waist and pulling her close. Elayne stepped back, but there was nowhere for her to go. She was good and caught.

"You're supposed to be leaving." Her hands were on his chest, but the push she delivered was ineffectual. Or maybe it was hesitant.

"I'm not going anywhere."

"You were supposed to be headed back to the Army."

"Air Force," Aldo corrected. "My contract is up."

"Sign a new one."

"No."

"Glad to know it's not just my paperwork you won't sign."

He grinned down at her mouth. There was the M. He wanted to make Elayne Jade say more M words. Like *my* and *Matthews* and *mine.* She would be a Matthews soon, and he was going to kiss those lips that would belong to him.

"Look, Aldo…" she sighed, still pressing against his chest, but not enough to actually dislodge him. "I need you to do something for me."

Aldo pulled her tighter, pressing his chest to hers. His head came down another inch closer to her lips. Just a little closer. "I would do anything for you."

That won him another shocked glance. This time her lips parted, forming a perfectly shaped O. It was his new favorite look of hers. Aldo wondered what O words he could get her to say. He should start with a simple *ohhh* and go from there. He bet a kiss would elicit that sound from her perfect mouth.

It took her a moment to compose herself. Plenty of time for him to make another sneak attack. But he didn't want this to sneak up on her. He wanted her to come to him.

"I need you to come to dinner with me," she said finally.

"Done."

"It's with the police chief."

"My new boss."

"So you really are joining the police force? You're staying here? Why?"

Aldo didn't answer with words. Instead, he reached for a strand of her hair. Elayne watched him from the corner of her eye. They both stared at the hair he twined around his index finger.

Slowly, she backed away from him, letting the coil of hair unfurl from his finger. But she still looked caught. He let her go, secure in the fact that he'd won this first battle and was close to winning the war with his nemesis.

He'd fallen long ago for Elayne Jade. Now it was her turn.

"I'll pick you up for dinner," he said.

"Fine." She turned to go, but then turned back. "They think we're engaged, not married. Don't tell them the truth."

"I won't," he promised. "You have my word."

CHAPTER TWELVE

"You're going on a date?"

"It's not a date." Elayne tossed aside the skirt she'd picked up. It's what she wore when she wanted guys to buy her a drink. It never failed. It was far from the school guidance counselor look of skirts that went below the knee at the bottom and provided space for a prim blouse to be tucked into the top.

No, this skirt molded to her backside, leaving lots of space to take hold of the imagination. Meaning it made men hope, wonder, and pray. It also stopped way above her knees, just shy of mid-thigh. If she wore this, Aldo might think he had a prayer of a chance to...

To what? He'd already managed to get his ring

on her finger. Was he expecting that to gain him access to full marital rights?

Elayne scoffed at the thought. Well, she opened her mouth to make a scoffing sound. That dismissive vibration started at the back of her throat. But when it rolled off her tongue, it was nothing but a breathy sigh that was a prayer of her own.

She needed patience. She needed strength. Most of all, Elayne needed understanding.

She needed to understand why Aldo had done this. And done it sober. She still couldn't figure out his angle in this farce.

Putting back the free-drinks dress, because Lord knew she wasn't drinking again anytime this century, Elayne pulled out a pale, prim dress that covered her collarbones and kissed her calves. For all intents and purposes, this dress would serve as armor. She had to be on her guard for anything Aldo Matthews might say or do tonight.

"If it's not a date, then what is it?" asked Kailyn.

"Dinner with some work colleagues."

"You don't work with Aldo."

"He was invited by my colleague, and he's picking me up to conserve gas."

"Hmmm," Kailyn hummed, bouncing one crossed leg over the other while she sat in a plush chair next to Elayne's closet. "Your husband is taking you out to dinner with some friends from work. It sounds like a date."

Elayne threw up her hands, exasperated. She was done trying to explain this to her sister. With her hands up in the air, she let go of the armor dress. It fell into a heap on the floor.

From her short stint in the foster system, Elayne had learned it was her responsibility to clean up after herself and not to rely on adults. She carried that lesson over and into her adoptive parents' house. Dishes were never left out overnight and typically were washed and cleaned right after the meal. The counters were always spotless, the floors always gleamed. So technically, her closet floor should have been clean enough to not transfer any dirt or dust to the dress.

But Elayne decided it was better to be cautious. So back on the hanger the pale, conservative armor dress went. Which left her looking again at the free-drinks dress. Maybe she could pare it with a cardigan to dampen its power?

"You're wearing that?" said Kailyn.

"What's wrong with this?" Elayne asked, holding up the black dress to her form. She'd been wrong. The dress was a little higher on her thigh than she remembered.

"Nothing." Kailyn grinned. "It's just that I borrowed it a few nights ago for a date with Mateo, and he couldn't keep his eyes—or his hands—off me."

Elayne stepped into the garment and pulled the fabric up her body. The zipper glided smoothly up her side until the dress fit her like a second skin. She stepped in front of the mirror. Wow, that hem had risen even higher.

"If you want an annulment, I don't think that's the way to go."

"Of course I want an annulment. I still don't know what got into me agreeing to marry that man. Or what a pastor or judge must have been thinking when he saw the state I was in to think I was giving consent."

Elayne smoothed her hand down the dress. She definitely wouldn't have to buy a single drink the way she was looking tonight. Any man who caught sight of her might decide he was punch drunk based on the amount of cleavage she had on display.

"But I'm getting invited places I didn't have access to because of this." Elayne held up the ring she'd put back on her finger. "I'm just going to secure my place in the guidance office, secure my ideas with the head counselors. Aldo and I can still handle the annulment quietly. The Mosses just think we're engaged. After the paperwork is filed, we can call off our engagement, and by then I'll already have what I want."

Her twin nodded sagely, but Elayne knew better than to think Kailyn was agreeing with her —or letting her off the hook.

"Meaning you'll lie. Even though you hate liars."

That she did. And Aldo Matthews was a liar. "I'm not lying. I'm just not giving all the information."

Kailyn opened her mouth like she was going to say more, but that's when the doorbell rang.

Elayne snatched the pale cardigan from a hanger. She pulled it around her shoulders, knowing full well that it wouldn't dampen the power of the free-drinks dress. Not with her long legs still on display.

She slipped into shoes and went to open the door before Kailyn could get there. Elayne pulled open the door to see Aldo standing on the other side. She had intended to keep her forward motion going right out of the door and into his car, but she came to an abrupt halt. Her body might've stopped moving, but her heart slammed into her rib cage and kept moving as though it were racing to him.

Elayne had never let herself notice before just how devastatingly handsome Aldo was. Chiseled jaw. Lips lifted in a perpetual grin of mischief. Those eyes—they'd often held her in place when they were younger and fighting. But during those times, she'd been fuming, seeing red. Now she was caught in the golden flecks of hazel sparkling down on her.

"Wow," Aldo breathed. "You just took my breath away."

And he had just stolen hers. The thief. He was a liar and a thief. A devastatingly handsome thief who stole any response. A liar whose approving gaze dared her to blink first.

"You've always been a knockout, Elayne, but tonight..." Aldo let the sentence trail off as his gaze took the slow route down her body. The cardigan could have been a flimsy piece of lace the way he looked through it.

"Don't do that," she demanded.

"Do what?"

"You don't have to be nice to me right now. No one's watching."

"How should I behave when no one's watching us, Elayne?"

The way he said her name, it came out husky. Had he ever called her by her name before? Or had it always been Andy?

Andy, like his mother's favorite doll. Mateo had admitted to Kailyn that those dolls were his prized possession, just as she was to him. It should have changed the context for Elayne, but Aldo had never divulged that particular fact. For all she knew, he could've hated the dolls.

"You said you wanted there to be peace between us." Aldo took a step toward her, crowding her space. If there was a line in the sand, he'd definitely crossed it. "This is me being friendly. Can you do the same?"

"I'm not sure how to be nice to you."

"Just don't bite my head off, and we'll call that a start."

"Me?" Elayne pointed at her chest. "Bite your head off?" She turned her index finger on him. "You always start it."

"Because you're cute when I ruffle your feathers."

Once again, she had the wind knocked out of her. She wasn't sure how to deal with this man like this when he was being… Was he being charming? Was he flirting? Elayne felt drunk, and she hadn't touched any alcohol since that night at the hotel.

"Can we just go?"

"Yes, dear."

"Don't call me that."

"Okay, sweetheart."

She glared at him as he walked her to the car. The man was impossible. And she wasn't sure how she was going to survive this night.

CHAPTER THIRTEEN

"**R**emember, they just think we're engaged and not married yet."

"Okay, babe."

"So don't let it slip that we're actually married."

"Sure, dumpling."

"Or that we're getting an annulment."

"Whatever you want, angel."

"Because we *are* getting an annulment."

"If you think so, love."

Yeah, Aldo liked that last one. Calling Elayne Jade *love* rolled off his tongue effortlessly. *Babe* had sounded a bit too smarmy. He'd almost chuckled as he'd said *dumpling. Angel* was definitely not the one, as the woman had proven time and again that she had the devil firmly planted on one shoulder. But Aldo liked that side of Elayne.

Love? Yeah, that one would stick. That would be his endearment for the woman who would one day be his wife.

"Will you take this seriously, Aldo?"

"I take the two of us very seriously, Elayne."

She blinked, her eyes fluttering like a bird's. Then she swallowed hard, like she'd tasted some-thing bitter. Right, she didn't want him calling her by her name.

"Sorry, love."

"Don't call me that either. I'm not someone you love."

Aldo wanted to dispute that. He had loved Elayne Jade since the first time he'd seen her when they were in foster care together. He hadn't understood what those sensations of his heart skipping a beat, him losing his breath, that grumble in his belly, and feeling hot all over, meant.

As a grown man, he understood it now. He'd seen it happen to each of his brothers when they were in the same space as the women they loved. That same dummy look that coated their features when they spoke about their girlfriends or wives.

He'd worn that same look every single time he'd come face to face with Elayne.

He'd thought that, as his nemesis, she would be his downfall. Now he knew he'd fallen that first day, and he'd be at her feet for the rest of their lives.

But she didn't look at him that way. Not exactly. She was still fighting. She hadn't noticed that he had surrendered in their game.

"We're supposed to be in love," he said. "It would make sense to other people, especially other couples, that I have an endearment that I call you."

Elayne chewed at her lip. Aldo turned green. Jealousy rose in his throat and coated his tongue. He wanted to take over and bite that plump lip himself.

"Would you rather me call you Andy?"

She let go of her bottom lip. Her top lip slammed down, like a jail cell shutting him out. Aldo only barely stopped himself from leaning down and kissing those lips apart. *Soon,* he told himself.

Soon.

But why not now? They were playing the role of smitten newlyweds. It would make sense for him to touch her, and kiss her, and whisper in her ear. As if he were a green light incarnate, Chief Moss and his wife appeared at the door to the restaurant.

It was the perfect opportunity to show affection for his bride. Aldo, who had always been told he had poor impulse control, decided to take advantage.

His hand circled around Elayne's back. She bristled as he got close. Then froze as he got even closer. Her lips parted, but he knew that particular move of hers. She wasn't about to encourage him. She was about to admonish him, to start an argument.

There was a part of Aldo that wanted to watch her mouth move this close as she ripped into him. But the desire to taste those lips that had always fascinated him was too great.

"Careful," he soothed. "The Mosses are right in front of us."

He caught Elayne's intake of breath. It was as close to a green light as he needed. Aldo brushed his lips against Elayne's, ensuring that she would take in the air he breathed. Turnabout was fair play. Now maybe she'd feel some of the lightheadedness he endured whenever she was in his presence.

Aldo kept the kiss light. He had to. His instincts were to gorge himself on her. Just this slight sweet taste was already heating his blood to dangerous levels.

Elayne's lips quivered beneath his. Aldo touched his tongue to the summit of her mouth. Her sigh sounded to his ears like surrender, and he fell.

Or at least he felt like he was falling. Aldo plummeted down the twin peaks he'd dreamed about for nearly two decades. That divot in Elayne Jade's upper lip was where he found heaven.

Elayne leaned in, seeking more of him without realizing it. He gave himself to her. Showing her that there wasn't a single iota of resistance to him, to them, inside of him. She had always been the inescapable agent of his downfall: his nemesis.

Aldo deepened the kiss. Just enough to give them both a taste of the bliss he knew they would create when she finally accepted what was between them. He nibbled at the center of her upper lip, and it nearly brought him to his knees. The sound of a throat clearing, and then two throats clearing, and then a loud *ahem* brought him back from the brink.

"Do you remember us at that age, Jim?"

"I remember you couldn't keep your hands off me."

Mrs. Moss smacked her husband on the chest with the back of her hand. Captain Moss caught and held that hand, pressing his wife's fingertips to his lips.

Desire shot through Aldo. That's what he wanted with Elayne. To be gray and wizened and to capture her hand when she lashed out at him.

Because he knew she would lash out at him. It was their thing. It was his favorite thing about her. The way Elayne would get fired up, all of her attention focused on him and how to take him down.

"Seems like you didn't tell the little lady about taking the job at the force," said Chief.

"No, I wanted to surprise her." Aldo looked down at Elayne. She looked dazed and unsteady. Her gaze darted as though she was ready to bolt. Aldo's hold tightened.

"Sorry, I ruined that," said Mrs. Moss, a sheepish grin on her face as she took in the two of them.

"It was a happy surprise, wasn't it, my love?" Aldo kissed the cone of Elayne's ear.

She shuddered and had to swallow a few times

before she could answer. "It was a shock to learn you wouldn't be going back into a war zone."

Aldo nearly laughed. He loved that she could still rib him even while trying to play nice. He would never get bored with this woman as his wife.

"You proposed the night of the conference?" said Mrs. Moss. "I didn't even know you were there."

"I was attending a military contractor event hosted by the Purple Heart Ranch. I would've married Elayne that night. There were two pastors at the ranch."

"Pastors Patel and Vance." Captain Moss nodded. "Those are two good men. Married most of the men and women on the Purple Heart Ranch. Crazy about that zoning law."

Aldo played with Elayne's hair, running his fingers through it like he'd always wanted to. He'd go on couples' date after couples' date if it meant he had this kind of access to her. She was a captive right now, and he wasn't going to stop until she waved the white flag of surrender.

CHAPTER FOURTEEN

He was a convincing liar. Elayne would give him that. He almost had her fooled. The way he looked at her with those adoring eyes. The way his hand rested over the back of her chair, his thumb running lazy circles on her shoulders. She was half tempted to take the cardigan off to cool her heated skin.

But it was difficult to break away from his touch. From his gaze. From those kisses.

He kept sneaking in kisses. In her hair. At her temple. On her shoulder. On the back of her neck Now on each of the fingertips of her left hand. And she couldn't pull away.

Not if she wanted to keep up this farce. Because it was a farce.

Aldo was playing a game. He was always playing some form of the Dirty Dozens with her. Only this time she couldn't be sure if she was losing or he was winning. What was the difference?

"It was love at first sight for me."

That statement should have infuriated her. It was all lies from the first word to the emphatic period. Aldo had hated her the first time he'd set eyes on her.

Hadn't he?

"I never knew how to talk to her," he continued. "She was so smart and so pretty. She reminded me of a doll."

Her breath caught. *Don't say it.* If he said the name Andy, she was going to lose it.

Hazel eyes met hers. That smirk lifted at one corner, as though he knew exactly what she was thinking. That single word was between them. But even though he smirked, it didn't look like he was joking or being mean.

Elayne knew Aldo's mean face. Or at least she thought she did. How could he be saying such kind, romantic words with that mouth that had always caused her pain?

His hand lifted to her neck. His thumb rubbed

at the spot just behind her ear. It was soothing, caring. The kind of move that a loved one would use to tend to a wound. Instead of making Elayne feel better, it muddled her mind.

"You were both in the foster care system?" Dr. Moss asked.

Elayne couldn't answer. She forgot how to form words with Aldo making those pacifying circles behind her ear. Aldo nodded and spoke for them both.

"We both got adopted by the best couples in this town. We both want to give back to it. That's why, after years of military service, I'm joining the police force. And Elayne has great ideas for helping the kids in Honor Valley. Don't you, love?"

That was her cue. They hadn't discussed the need to highlight Elayne's professional traits at this dinner. But somehow he knew, and he'd served her up on a platter to her boss. But Elayne was still stuck on the endearment he'd chosen for her.

Love.

She had to remind herself that she wasn't his love. That he wasn't in love with her. It was all a farce. Just like their marriage.

But why? Why had he done it? What was he

doing now? Besides making her feel ooey and gooey inside.

"Elayne?" asked Dr. Moss.

Elayne cleared her throat. She'd rehearsed what she was going to say during this dinner. She'd written reports about the counseling programs and protocols she wanted to implement in the high school to help this new generation, who seemed more stressed-out and anxious than any that had come before.

She leaned forward and presented her ideas. All the while, she felt Aldo's hand resting at the back of her chair. He wasn't rubbing behind her ear anymore. Now his fingers played in her hair. Hair he'd made fun of as a kid. Why would he be gazing at it as though he couldn't take it in enough?

"These are really good ideas," said Dr. Moss. "We should bring them up at the next meeting."

Elayne had tried that. But she'd been shoved to the bottom of the agenda, then promised they would take it up at the next meeting, only to be shoved down again. She didn't remind Dr. Moss of any of this. She was being heard now, and it was all thanks to Aldo.

Aldo, the man who insisted on paying the bill for all of them. Aldo, the man who rested his hand at the small of her back as they said goodbye to the Mosses. Aldo, the man who handed her into the passenger seat of his car and waited for her to buckle up before climbing into the driver's side.

Elayne sat back in the passenger seat. She felt like a passenger in her own life. She wasn't sure which direction she was going in. Aldo had accepted another double date invitation with the Mosses for the weekend. She should have declined. Their marriage would be annulled by then. Already, tonight she had gotten what she wanted: She'd be placed on the counseling program's agenda and be heard. She didn't need to use Aldo anymore. So why was he still here?

"Why are you doing this?"

"Driving you home?"

"You know what I mean."

"Actually, I don't. There's more than one angle at work here, love."

"Stop calling me that. We're alone again."

"So when we're alone, you want me to call you Elayne."

"You're so frustrating."

Elayne slumped farther in the passenger seat, but when she did, her dress rode even higher up her thighs. A glance to her left told her that Aldo wasn't looking at her legs. He was grinning at her face.

"Your face goes red when you get frustrated. It's always fascinated me. When we were kids, I used to think that's why you had red hair, like a blush. I thought you had magic in you and that you could turn your whole person red if I just got you riled enough."

"Is that why you picked on me? To see if I'd change colors?"

He'd pulled onto the main street as he spoke. The light turned from green to yellow. Aldo had time to roll through the changing light before it turned red, but he slowed the car to a stop.

"Picking on you, as you call it, was the only way you'd talk to me."

"That's not…"

The red light changed to red. Across the street, the white pedestrian sign blinked, letting walkers know it was safe to cross.

"I tried to be nice to you a couple of times," he mused. "It never worked. You either ignored me or yelled at me. You never ignored me when I poked at you. So I kept poking."

The walking man changed to numbers in a countdown. Time was almost up for the people in the middle of the street to make their way across before vehicles once again claimed the open road.

Elayne opened her mouth and closed it again. She ran through scenario after scenario of her time going toe to toe with Aldo Matthews. Had he ever said a kind word to her? She honestly couldn't remember.

She was still sifting through her memories when the car pulled to another stop. They had arrived at her house, and she couldn't remember the ride. He hadn't said another word to her. It was the longest time she'd heard the man be quiet.

Elayne reached for the door handle. The look of displeasure Aldo gave her made her snatch her hand back from the handle. As he climbed out of the driver's side and walked around the front of the car, Elayne realized he'd never looked at her like that before. With dark displeasure.

Aldo had always had a slight smirk on his face. His eyes were always bright and excited as he gazed down. Had he? Did he? Did he enjoy fighting with her? Did he think of their relationship as an actual game? One that he played for fun and enjoyment? One that he looked forward to playing with her? Not with the dread she felt every time she rounded a corner and saw him lying in wait.

When Aldo opened the door, she took the hand he offered her. She had to. Elayne couldn't tell which way was up or down. Left or right. Right or wrong.

"Should I kiss you goodnight, Elayne?"

Elayne blinked. They were standing under the porch light, but she didn't need any added illumination to see the desire or the excitement in his eyes. Was this part of the game?

"Do you want me to kiss you again, love?"

Finally, a question she knew the answer to. Though the answer surprised her so much that she wouldn't let it pass her lips. So she bobbed her head instead.

As though he knew her struggles and reveled in them, he said, "Ask me to."

In the darkness, pride left her. Desire was the only thing keeping her warm. That and Aldo's hand resting lighting on her hip. "Kiss me."

"Ask me nicely."

That broke the spell—mostly. Elayne's eyes flashed up at him. All she saw was the bright glare of sharp, white teeth as Aldo chuckled at her.

That was him. That was the devilish boy from her childhood. The bully from her teen years. How could she think for a second that he—

Aldo's mouth crashed down on hers. Not just his mouth on her lips; his hands were on her too. One cupping her chin, fingers tangling in her hair. The other sat at her lower back, pulling her closer until there was no space between them. It was a full-on assault, and Elayne immediately threw up the flag of surrender.

How could she not? She had no other choice. He had knocked down every single one of her defenses, leaving her spinning in circles so he could perform this sneak attack.

Aldo didn't kiss her. He ate at her mouth. Like he hadn't eaten the meal on the table and some off her plate less than a half hour ago. He devoured her, deepening that kiss and taking more than she thought she had to give him. He left her breathless and starving for more.

"Go inside," he growled when he broke the kiss.

Elayne's head might be foggy, her defenses might be down, but she was very clear on what she wanted to happen next. "You know, we are married. So…"

She let that sentence dangle as she threaded her arms around his neck. Aldo took a deep breath, then a second before disentangling her.

"Go inside, Elayne."

The starvation she'd just experienced turned to an instant pain. There it was. That was his game. To get her riled up and leave her wanting more.

He hadn't changed. He would never change. And he'd won again. Elayne opened the door and slammed it in his face. The slam echoed inside the hollowness in her chest.

CHAPTER FIFTEEN

Shouts and squeals roused Aldo from his sleep. The sounds disoriented him because they were high-pitched and youthful. Not the grunts and body sounds of grown men in close quarters. He wasn't on the base, but he wasn't some place unfamiliar to him.

"You're taking forever."

"Other people need to get ready for school."

Yes, those wails he remembered. For years, Aldo had risen late in the morning in the foster home to a smelly shared bathroom as boys got ready for the day. In the military, morning rituals had been more regimented, but the sounds and smells were much the same. There was nothing like the bickering of siblings to get a man to roll out of bed on the wrong side.

Aldo had spent his formative years in the bunkhouse with his five brothers as they got ready each morning for school, chores, or church. Those same sounds and smells could be heard and sniffed every morning on the Flying Cross Ranch, which only had three bathrooms and at least seven male bodies who had to get ready at the crack of dawn.

Father Matthews was always the first up, and his sons would never hear a peep from him as he went about his morning rituals. He was always at the breakfast table or out on the ranch working by the time the boys wiped the crust from the corners of their eyes. Aldo was usually the last of his brothers to rise and was often met with a cold shower, nearly depleted toiletries, and no clean towels.

In that moment, he preferred the sounds and smells of the base.

"I need this bathroom to get ready," said the deepest male voice. It was Denny, the eldest of the new foster kids inhabiting the bunkhouse where there was only one bathroom and limited hot water.

Denny's voice mingled with a high-pitched

feminine voice, who could've been his sassy little sister Daria or the wise-beyond-her-years LaTisha. Aldo would put his money on the voice of contention being Daria. LaTisha would've been like his dad and risen at an optimal time to not have to deal with any bickering.

The bickering was coming from across the hall in the main house where Aldo was bundled up on the pull-out couch in the family room. The space was Aldo's until he decided if he was going to build a place of his own on the land or find a place in town.

Mateo had found and leased an apartment the day after Aldo returned from his trip. It was the first time they'd lived apart outside of the military. It was also the first time that Aldo didn't feel like a piece of himself was missing.

He didn't want Mateo's sharp eyes on him right now, questioning and judging him. No, Aldo wanted Elayne Jade's green gaze to do that.

This morning, while World War III waged across the hall, Aldo wished he'd taken Elayne up on her offer to come inside her house. He wouldn't be hearing adolescent bombs going off right now. He'd be hearing those little moans she made at the back of her throat when he kissed her.

Aldo groaned just thinking about it. He threw his hand over his head. And there it was. He caught just a hint of that spicy scent of hers: hot cinnamon on a cold evening.

He inhaled deeply, wishing his nose was buried in the crook of her neck. Wishing his fingers were tangled in those red strands. Wishing his teeth were nibbling on the divot at her upper lip.

Soon, he promised himself. He'd done so much wrong in their relationship over the years. This time, he was going to do everything right. That started with not taking her offering last night. Not when there was a big, fat lie between them.

True, Aldo was harboring a lie about his relationship with Elayne. But if he played his cards right, that lie about them being married could become a reality. With that wishful prayer, Aldo rose for the day and promptly fell back on his behind.

A quart of cologne wafted out of the bathroom before Denny did. Aldo teared up, looking with desperation at the window latch on the other side of the family room.

"What?" asked Denny.

"Did you spill the bottle on yourself?"

"Too much?" Denny asked, raising his forearm

to his nose. In true teenager fashion, with a young nose that was immune to most noxious fumes, the kid didn't even flinch.

"You trying to impress a girl or something?" Aldo asked.

He flinched at that, his broadening shoulders huddling in on himself. "Yeah."

Aldo nodded slowly, considering his words. "Girls like subtly. When it comes to cologne, anyway. You want to give them just a hint and then make them lean in."

Denny nodded slowly, considering Aldo's words. He reached back into the bathroom and rubbed a washcloth over his neck and wrists. "What else do they like?"

"Shouldn't you be talking to Charlie about this?"

Denny rolled his eyes. The movement caused another waft of cologne to singe Aldo's nose hairs. But Aldo could understand the eye roll.

Charlie had only loved one girl all his life. Any dating advice he might come up with in his total lack of game would be to follow the object of affection around until she threw up her hands and gave in. That method had taken Charlie nearly twenty years to finally get a ring on Savy's finger.

There had only been one girl for Aldo too. He'd gotten his ring on Elayne's finger in a very different manner. "Have you told her you like her?"

Denny shrugged. "I haven't even talked to her. Savy says I should compliment her."

"Compliments don't always work." Aldo had tried to compliment Elayne, and she would always turn it around on him. Or worse, she'd ignore him completely. "You gotta say something to get under her skin. Make her stop and take notice of you. That's not always the nice thing."

"You're telling me to be mean?"

"Not mean exactly. I—"

"I heard about that tactic on a YouTube Channel. It was called Chad Bro. This guy Chad talked about how he got a lot of women's numbers."

"I don't think you should listen to a guy who calls himself Chad Bro."

"I hear you. Why would I want a girl's number when I can just DM her social media handle?"

"Wait? What?"

"Thanks, Uncle Aldo. I knew you were the best guy to talk to about this. You're the only one who isn't married or engaged."

"No, I am…" He was what? Not married. Not exactly engaged.

"I thought Uncle Mateo said you were getting an annulment."

"No one's getting anything annulled."

"I don't see your wife here with you."

"Yet."

Denny looked doubtful, but he nodded, hands up as he walked backward down the hall toward the front door.

Aldo dressed quickly, preparing to go in for his first day of training for the police academy. His father was rocking on the porch when he came out. Aldo rested a hand on the old man's shoulder. Father Matthews didn't need to turn to see which of his sons was at his back. Even though he'd raised six boys, two of them twins, he could be resting with his eyes closed and know who had approached him.

"Denny has a point. I would like to meet this wife of yours."

"You heard that from all the way out here?"

"I have the hearing of an elephant, son."

"I thought elephants had long memories."

"And big ears." Father Matthews grinned.

"She's not my wife," Aldo admitted. "Not yet."

Father Matthews turned a surprised gaze to his son. It was hard to catch the man off guard. It was usually Aldo who accomplished it.

"I proposed to her. But she was…" He didn't want to say that Elayne was drunk. That wouldn't make a good impression. "She didn't entirely agree at the moment. But you're going to meet her soon, and you're going to love her."

Father Matthews chuckled. "Never thought that it would take a heart attack to make all my boys come home and find love."

"Yeah, don't do that again."

"Don't worry, son. I won't. My heart is too full to skip a beat again."

CHAPTER SIXTEEN

"Have I told you how beautiful you are this morning?" said Mateo.

"Yes, but only about three times so far," said Kailyn.

Elayne made a face in her oatmeal. Mateo had come over for breakfast before seeing Kailyn off to work. This was after he'd brought her twin sister home late last night. It had barely been seven hours that they'd been apart. And here they were, back together again, making gooey eyes at each other.

It was too early for this.

Elayne needed her sister's attention. They hadn't had a chance to talk about Elayne's disastrous, confusing, pulse-pounding, heart-stopping, not quite a *date,* but definitely *something* with Aldo Matthews. And then there was that soul-stirring kiss. Followed by the bucket of ice water dumped over her head in the form of a rejection.

Glaring at Mateo, who had the misfortune of sharing facial features with Aldo, Elayne thought of what she wanted to do to Aldo. She wanted to slam the door in his face again. Preferably while his perfect nose was in the way.

"What did my brother do?"

Elayne blinked, looking up at Mateo. Though his features were similar to Aldo's, she had to admit that the two men looked entirely different. There were smile lines at the corner of Mateo's eyes. His hazel eyes were a softer shade too, with less sparks of gold around the edges. Mateo also held on to her sister's hand, twining their fingers and stroking Kailyn's bare ring finger.

Elayne ran her thumb over her left ring finger. Aldo's ring was there. She had no idea why she was still wearing it. She should have flung it across the room last night. But she'd spent too long staring at it in the moonlight.

She still didn't remember accepting it. Not

entirely. There was the hazy memory of Aldo grinning at her as he held up the sparkling gem.

He hadn't gotten down on one knee. That she knew she would definitely remember. Seeing her greatest foe fall to his knees was a dream her brain would never let go of. He'd been standing toe to toe with her when he'd asked the question, Elayne was sure of it.

"It was our mother's ring," said Mateo, nodding to the band on Elayne's finger. "I took the dolls. He kept the ring."

Aldo had told her that. Hadn't he? She vaguely remembered him talking about his mother.

"Your eyes were throwing daggers at me a moment ago," said Mateo. "But I'm not my brother."

"I know that," Elayne sighed. But she wasn't about to explain to her sister or Aldo's brother that she was upset about being turned down by him last night. "I don't blame you for your brother's actions. I never have. You've always been decent."

"Even if silent?" Mateo said with a wince.

Kailyn's fingers tightened around his. He looked up at her through his long lashes. Kailyn had often remarked that Mateo had stood by when

Aldo and Elayne got into it. The fact that Mateo would never step into their arguments always bothered Kailyn. It looked like Mateo had resolved not to hold his tongue any longer.

"My brother's been obsessed with you since we were kids," he said, turning his attention back to Elayne.

"Obsessed?" Elayne's hand rose to her mouth as the word left her lips. Her breath blew through her fingers as though she could capture that one word and examine it. It was such a farfetched notion.

"Well, what would you call it? He would always seek you out. Every day in school, he would find a way to talk to you. What else would you call it?"

That made no sense. If he actually liked Elayne, he would've found something nice to say to her at least once.

I tried to be nice to you a couple of times. It never worked. You either ignored me or you yelled at me. You never ignored me when I poked at you. So I kept poking.

Aldo had kept poking. And she'd kept arguing with him—talking to him.

"He tricked me into marrying him." Elayne held up her left hand in evidence. The gems winked back at her, twinkling in the early sunlight like they were dancing on her finger.

"I know I don't know you well, Elayne," Mateo was saying, "but I have never seen you do anything you don't want to do. Especially where my brother is concerned."

Elayne glared, but Mateo was unperturbed. Right then, he looked exactly like his twin. The corner of his mouth was raised in a smirk. The light in his gaze challenged her to disagree with him.

"Savy said something interesting the other week," said Kailyn, but she was turned to Mateo as she spoke. "She said boys tug on the hair of girls until they know how to behave."

Mateo nodded with a grin. "Sounds about right." He reached up and tugged on Kailyn's hair.

"You don't have to do that anymore," she giggled. "Now you know exactly what to say to me."

"I do," he said. "I'm so hopelessly in love with you, Kailyn Jade. You're going to have to save me."

"Don't worry, I've got your back." Kailyn leaned in for a kiss. For a moment—make that two minutes—the two lovebirds completely forgot Elayne was standing there.

"I'm headed out," Elayne said, dumping her

half-eaten oatmeal into the trash. "You can get a ride from your hopeless love."

"Say hi to your husband for me," called Kailyn, arms still wrapped around Mateo's neck.

"He's not going to be my husband much longer. Besides, I'm not seeing him today."

"You saw him last night."

Elayne nodded.

"And the day before."

Elayne exhaled sharply from her nose, not liking where this was headed.

"And you spent the weekend together right before you got married."

"This marriage won't last," said Elayne, checking in her bag for the annulment papers.

"I hope it does," said Mateo. "You're a really good influence on my brother. I've seen changes in him I never expected."

There was a part of Elayne that wanted to ask what changes. But the more vocal part, the part that was still reeling from Aldo's rejection after that scorching kiss, was louder. It responded to the hopelessly devoted couple by storming out the front door.

The smell of teen spirit, which was a mix of too-sweet perfumes and noxious cologne, hit her the moment she walked into the school's front entrance. The buzzing sound of adolescents all speaking excitedly over one another dulled her own thoughts as she walked down the hall. But the ghosts of times past decided it would visit her today.

Near the sophomore hall of lockers, Elayne remembered an encounter with Aldo when he'd told her her hair looked like carrots. Moving beyond that, she turned the corner near the junior hall when he'd witness her first boyfriend dump her.

The dumping had happened after Aldo had punched Darius Cox in the face. Months later, Elayne had counted her blessings after a couple of girls got in a fight over who was really Darius' girlfriend. As she'd listened into the catfight, she'd noted that at least one of them had been dating Darius at the same time he'd been hitting on her.

Had Aldo known what Darius was up to? Had that been the reason he'd told her that she couldn't date Darius?

My brother's been obsessed with you since we were kids.

Elayne still couldn't wrap her brain around Mateo's words. She couldn't wrap her brain around Aldo's proposal. She couldn't get her brain to function very much at all these days.

"Anybody ever tell you that your hair looks like Medusa's snakes?"

Elayne's gasps mingled with the lanky girl who the insult was aimed at. Standing between the lockers, Elayne spied a brown-skinned girl—Keisha, she thought the girl's name was. The glistening coils of her dreadlocks hung down her back and across her shoulders. She pushed them all behind her neck as she averted her gaze from the bully.

Elaine recognized that kid, too. It was one of the new generations of Matthews. Denny.

Denny's grin dropped as he watched Keisha turn away from him with a brush of her index finger at the corner of her eyes. He held up his hands as though to stop her, but immediately dropped them when he saw Elayne.

"I don't understand," he said to Elayne as though he was the affronted party. "Why did she get upset?""

"What made you say those things? In what world would you think that's okay?"

Denny looked truly confused. He crossed his arms and chewed at his lower lip, his gaze still down the hall where Keisha was ducking into the girl's bathroom. "I just wanted her to talk to me. My uncle said sometimes the only way girls will talk to you is if you're mean to them."

"Which uncle?"

"Your husband."

CHAPTER SEVENTEEN

Aldo loved nothing more than a day of hard work, clear instructions, and a job well done. He'd accomplished all three of those things on his first day of training at the police academy.

He'd been worried that police work wouldn't give him the same thrill, the same feeling of service and satisfaction as his military career had. There was an adrenaline rush to being in the air, to sleeping close to a combat area, to rushing into a battle zone with your fellow soldiers at your side. But learning the protocols and procedures of how to protect the people in his small community felt even bigger than protecting all the citizens in his country. This was more personal.

"Good work today, Matthews," said his new boss.

Being that it was a small town, his training was being held at the local community college. There were only three other cadets at the desks with Aldo. At first Aldo had balked at being put back in a classroom. But the lessons on how to handle domestic violence calls and child abuse cases made him sit forward.

Back during his time in foster care, he had witnessed the aftermath of those two things combined, but he'd been too young to do anything about it. Overseas in war zones, he'd witnessed them happening before his eyes, but his hands had been diplomatically tied then. Today, he was being given the skills to make a difference.

"Thank you, sir," Aldo said to Chief Moss. "I'm eager to get started. Even more, I feel this is what I'm supposed to be doing in this next phase of my life."

The chief grinned at him with a satisfied head bob. "I had a good time last night. Shirley and I would love to see you and the missus again." Moss held up his hand in apology. "Sorry, I mean your fiancée. Though you two sure act like an old married couple."

It was on the tip of Aldo's tongue to come clean, tell his new superior that Elayne was neither his wife nor his fiancée. His lips wouldn't form the words. Not when his heart flatly refused the notion that Elayne wasn't his.

So Aldo said nothing. All he could do was force a weak smile and nod. Chief Moss didn't appear to notice anything out of order. He gave Aldo a slap on his back and sent him out into the early evening with a grin on his face.

Aldo's grin widened when he saw Elayne leaning against his car. His mouth opened, ready to tell her every feeling that raged to the surface. Each and every one of them was about her.

His heart sped up. Skipped a beat. Only to race forward again. It didn't bother him in the slightest to know that this was how he was going to die: from a cardiac arrest over his devotion to this woman.

His head swiveled left and right, bobbing up and down, trying to take her all in at once. She wore a prim skirt, colorless blouse, and pale cardigan. She looked every bit the matronly guidance counselor preparing to shepherd the wayward youth of his generation. Aldo knew exactly where he wanted to be guided.

"Hey, love," he drawled as he came within earshot of her. "Ready for me to come home?"

Elayne had been looking down at the ground. Her lips had been moving, her features fierce. Much as she'd looked when he seen her rehearsing for a debate in English class. She'd won every argument during that lesson. Now she looked up at him, startled.

Aldo's gaze was latched onto her mouth. Her lips had parted when she looked up, making a perfect O shape. Her lips were usually compressed in that exaggerated M shape that he loved so much.

The O was stunning. It was also the perfect shape for kissing.

Elayne backed up from him. When her back came flush to his car, she startled again, realizing she had nowhere to go. The O shape returned briefly before her lips pursed into an M.

"You made it perfectly clear you didn't want to go home with me," she said.

Aldo crowded her into the car, boxing her in with his big body. Every warrior instinct in him told him to pounce. His prey was weak, and she had no escape. But he didn't want Elayne as docile prey. He wanted her to be the passionate predator alongside him.

"Didn't you?" she demanded.

Her eyes flicked down to the ground. They took a full breath before they rose back to meet his. Elayne backed down from a staring contest with him. Aldo didn't like the uncertainty he saw on her face. So he leaned in and kissed the corner of her eyelid.

Hot cinnamon heated him under his collar as her breath of surprise blasted against his neck. Her hands came up in front of his chest. They fluttered between them, like a bird uncertain of where to land.

"You think I don't want to come home with you?"

When he looked down, her eyes were dazed, unfocused. Her cheeks were flushed a beautiful shade of pink. But the uncertainty was still there in her features.

"I drove around your block for two hours last night. I have calluses on my calluses from gripping the steering wheel so tightly so that I wouldn't bang on your door."

Slowly, the uncertainty began to melt away. Her throat, which still was that warm shade of pink, worked as she swallowed a few times. Her eyes narrowed, but not in the defiant way she always looked at him. Confusion tipped her lashes.

"I'm not coming into your house until you stop believing I'm the big bad wolf."

Her gaze widened. The determined M came back to her lips. She leaned away from him, pressing herself back into the car. "Well, then you need to stop terrorizing little kids."

The woman always caught him off guard, and he loved every second of being knocked off-kilter. "What are you talking about?"

"Did you tell Denny to be mean to a little girl?"

"Why?" Aldo tempted fate by brushing his thumb just under her lower lip. Surprisingly, his digit remained intact. "Did it work?"

"No." Elayne's lower lip trembled slightly. "She got upset."

"But she noticed him." Aldo rubbed just at the edge of the plumpest part of her bottom lip. "She talked to him."

Elayne had to swallow before she spoke, but she still didn't pull away from his touch. "He hurt her feelings."

"He'll make it better." Aldo kissed the right corner of her mouth. Then again on the left side.

"So it's true?"

Her lips were barely a breath from his. He could've claimed her mouth, but he liked the position they were in too much. This was where he wanted to spend most of his time: right on the edge of having her.

"What's true, my love?"

When she spoke, her voice was barely a whisper and she wouldn't meet his gaze. "You've been mean to me all these years because… you liked me?"

Aldo waited in that space. He waited until she looked up at him so that she could see the truth rather than hear it.

Elayne swallowed a couple of times. Each compression of her lips brought their mouths closer and closer together, but Aldo refused to claim her. Not until she looked up.

Then she did. And she shoved him away.

Aldo stumbled back. Not from the force of the blow. From the shock of her rejection.

"That's the stupidest thing I've ever heard," she said, her voice back at full volume.

"Now who's name calling?"

"Why didn't you just try to talk to me, to be civil when we first met?"

"Because you ignored me. You looked at me like I was trash."

"I was a scared little girl. And you were fighting on that first day."

"I wouldn't have hurt you."

"Physically, no. My feelings, yes."

Aldo nodded, hanging his head. "I'll never do it again."

"Yes, you will."

Fair point. "I'll always kiss it better."

He took a step closer, his hands raised. She pursed her lips in that combative M. Aldo knew he had her. Sad, uncertain Elayne, he wasn't sure how to deal with. This Elayne who was ready for war, he knew exactly how to get past her defenses.

"Want me to kiss it better now, love?"

He wasn't even the slightest bit surprised when she sighed and admitted defeat with a weary "Yes."

Aldo pulled her close, but before his lips could descend and take the kiss his entire body was so hungry for, Elayne punched him in the chest. Right over his heart. The organ took it as a love tap and pressed harder against his chest to get at her.

"Ow, what was that for?"

"Don't tell any more boys to be mean to girls. It doesn't work."

"It worked for me."

"I'm still not sure I actually like you."

"Then come on a date with me. No other couples. No brothers or sisters or kids. Just you and me."

"That sounds dangerous."

"I'll protect you."

"From yourself?"

Aldo grinned, and then he claimed Elayne's mouth. All the while in his brain, he was mounting a defense to claim her heart so that his ring would stay on her finger permanently.

CHAPTER EIGHTEEN

Elayne entered the school building the next morning on Cloud Nine. She knew her head was in the clouds when she couldn't hear her heels clacking against the sticky linoleum floor. Her sister bounced beside her on an adjacent cloud.

"The Matthews boys," said Kailyn, her voice hushed in wonder.

"Who knew?" Elayne's voice held the same note of stunned awe.

"I did." Kailyn's look turned smug as they passed the cafeteria, where the breakfast rush was in full swing. "I felt something the first time I saw Mateo. We probably would've been together back in high school if it wasn't for you and Aldo's feud coming between us."

"It came between us too," Elayne admitted.

The sisters passed by the scene of Elayne's great breakup with Darius Cox. She saw Aldo standing over her ill-fated love with menace etched into his handsome face. She'd thought him the villain back then. Now she realized he was protecting her in the only way he knew how.

"But now that's over?" asked Kailyn. "The feud between you and Aldo, I mean."

"Yeah." Elayne blinked, the vision of Aldo from the past morphing to the man who had kissed her breathless outside the police precinct yesterday. "Yeah, I think it is."

Kailyn linked her arm through Elayne's. Elayne leaned into her sister. The two shared a secret smile that didn't hide that they were both falling stupidly in love.

The notion of love had Elayne tripping. Her heel came down hard on the linoleum. The sound was like a record scratch. But instead of coming to a halt, the music in her mind simply changed. It switched from a battle march to a love sonnet. Because Elayne wasn't storming forward any longer. She was falling in love.

"Hey, Keisha, wait up!"

"I don't want to talk to you, Denny. What you said to me the other day was inappropriate and offensive."

Both Kailyn and Elayne came to a halt at the far end of the hall where Denny was carefully, yet urgently, trailing behind the object of his affection. Keisha's long locks were hidden under a colorfully wrapped scarf piled on top of her head. Though one coiled tendril escaped on the side. She quickly tucked it behind her ear.

"I wasn't trying to be offensive," Denny was saying. "Well, I was, but I realize that was bad advice."

"I'm going to be late for class."

"I always thought Medusa was beautiful."

Keisha halted, her head whipping around to glare at him.

"In the Greek myths, it says Athena cursed her because she was so beautiful. Then in the Percy Jackson film, Medusa was played by Uma Thurman, who is crazy hot."

Keisha twirled the lock behind her ear as she regarded him.

"Then there's the actress who's going to play the new Little Mermaid. What's her name?"

"Halle Bailey."

"Yeah, her. She has locks, and she's really pretty."

Keisha's smile was tentative. Her gaze lowered and then rose to meet Denny's hopeful grimace.

"I just wanted to say I'm sorry," Denny said. "I didn't mean to hurt your feelings. I went about things the wrong way. Friends?"

Denny extended his hand, palm up. Keisha let go of her lock and placed her hand in his. The two stood there, gazing at each other with puppy dog eyes.

"Can I walk you to your class?" Denny asked.

Keisha nodded. He took her bag and walked side by side with her, stealing sheepish glances along the way. He still hadn't let go of her hand as they walked by Kailyn and Elayne.

"What was that?" asked Kailyn.

Elayne tilted her head to the side as she watched the two young people turn the corner. "That was history correcting itself."

"What?"

But Elayne only shook her head. She bussed her sister on the cheek and then headed right at the fork in the road that would take her to her office in the guidance suite. She plopped down in her chair, and the motion made the office chair spin halfway around. As her head spun, Elayne couldn't help thinking to herself how different her life might have been if she had behaved differently that first time she'd met Aldo.

The sound of her purse falling on the floor brought Elayne back around. Reaching for the spilled contents of her bag, she spied the annulment paperwork. She had forgotten the document was in there. Holding the pages in her hands, she was unsure what to do with them.

She could admit to herself that she was developing feelings for Aldo Matthews. But were they a lifetime's worth of feelings? A knock at her door brought her head up. The person standing in the door had Elayne's fingers fumbling to flip over the pages of the decree facedown on her desk.

"There you are," said Dr. Moss. "I wanted to tell you the good news myself. The committee took a look at your proposals—"

"What proposals?"

"The proposals you submitted."

Elayne opened her mouth and promptly shut it. The proposals she'd submitted months ago had been entirely ignored by the committee. She kept getting empty promise after empty promise that they would be placed on the agenda. At least the committee was making good on their word.

"The committee is interested in formally posting a position for a Mental Health and Wellness Counselor."

Elayne gasped, sitting up straight in her chair. This was the main proposal she'd been trying to impress upon the guidance committee for years. Her suggestion had always fallen on deaf ears, with members insisting that mental health wasn't the arena for school guidance.

"We think you're the right person for it, and we would like you to consider applying for the position."

"Thank you. Thank you." Elayne stood to shake Dr. Moss' hand. She kept saying the words on repeat. Even when she walked the woman to the door, she kept expressing her gratitude. This was the position she'd dreamed of having since college when she first realized the impact of stress and anxiety was growing not just in her generation, but in the one coming up after her. "I don't know how I could ever thank you enough for… for all of this."

"Just give me and Jim an invitation to your wedding. I hear the Silver sisters and Matthews brothers' weddings have been the talk of the town over the last few years."

"Wedding. Right."

"You probably have so much on your mind. A wedding to plan. Now a new job. And pretty soon..."

Dr. Moss patted Elayne's very flat belly. There was a hollow feeling there. But Elayne said nothing as she watched her boss leave the room.

She looked again at the turned-over annulment papers. She might not be ready for a wedding, and definitely not children of her own, but she also didn't care to sign the documents any longer. So Elayne tore them in half and let them fall into the wastebasket. The rest she would talk over with her husband.

Her husband? Elayne reached for the chair, letting her body slump into it. The more she thought about the H word, the more it felt right.

CHAPTER NINETEEN

Aldo rested his hip against the gate of the Jade home. He'd never been inside the ranch-style house that was painted a vibrant shade of blue. He'd only been past the white picket fence once. This afternoon he'd been invited.

The text from Elayne had come at the end of his training. She'd simply said *Come over.* It wasn't the first time Aldo had received a text like this from a woman. It was the first time it had been from the woman he wanted to come to. Now that he was here, exactly where he wanted to be, he wasn't sure how to get over the obstacle of the closed gate.

As if she heard his distress, the front door flung open. Elayne stood in the entryway. She wore an apron over her outfit. In bold block letters, the words on the apron read *Your opinion wasn't in the recipe.* Aldo chuckled at the phrase that was so her —at least when she was face to face with him.

His gaze continued down her lush body. The apron hung lower than her skirt, making her legs look bare. She wore no shoes, putting her purple-painted toes on display for him.

The sight of a nearly bare Elayne had Aldo clutching at the passenger side door. He was certain that if he let go, he'd launch himself at her. And where would that get him on his slow and steady campaign to win her over?

Elayne had been grinning at him, but her smile faltered. "You're not coming in?"

Aldo nodded and tried to swallow.

Elayne's features fell even more.

"No, no, I am coming in. I just—you just—" Aldo took a deep breath, let go of the passenger side door handle, and started again. "Elayne gotta warn a man before you do something like that."

He waved a hand in her general vicinity. Elayne looked down at her apron. Her bare toes flexed upwards. When she lifted her head, her features were colored with confusion.

"Something like what?"

Aldo couldn't answer. He'd gotten his wits back, and he knew exactly what to do. His addled brain remembered how to unlatch a gate. His military training kicked in, reminding him how to sneak up on an adversary.

But Elayne Jade was an adversary no longer. He prowled to her on sure steps, not hiding his intentions. Unlike him, Elayne didn't step back to grab at the front door handle. She stood still, waiting for him. The confusion morphed into certainty as she reached out a hand to him.

It was the first time she'd ever done anything like that. It was almost too much for Aldo to process. Almost.

Aldo launched himself at her. Or she flew into his arms. Either way, they met in the middle. He captured her upper lip and devoured it. She tugged his bottom lip into her mouth. He ate at that divot in the middle of her top lip. The taste was so sweet, so savory, so her. She made a sound at the back of her throat that suggested his opinion just might be welcome in the recipe they would make together.

He could've stood there in the doorway gorging himself on this woman, but a throat cleared behind him. Aldo didn't need to turn to know who had made the sound. It was exactly the sound his throat would've made if he'd had a death wish.

Aldo growled as he looked over Elayne's shoulder and saw his brother grinning at them in the foyer.

"Never thought I'd see this day," said Mateo as he walked up to his brother.

His brother's arm was slung around Kailyn. A face so similar to Elayne's but at the same time so very different grinned up. Then Kailyn turned that smile to Mateo, and the brightness went from one hundred to a one thousand-watt smile filled with love and adoration.

"What day is that?" asked Aldo.

"The day when I didn't have to step between you and Elayne Jade to counteract World War III."

"You'd be a fool to try to get between us right now." Aldo's fingers dug into Elayne's hip.

She'd turned around in his embrace, but she hadn't stepped out of it. Nor did she complain as his possessive fingers kept hold of her. She still looked dazed from the hungry kiss they'd just shared. She looked happy as she rested the back of her head against his shoulder.

"Are you going to feed me or what?" Aldo

growled as he kissed the top of her nose, then her cheek.

Elayne's lips spread into something soft and private just between them. With a sigh, she pushed off him. With a grunt, he let her go. Elayne reached for her sister. The two bent their heads together and giggled.

Mateo and Aldo stood watching after them. There was a dumfounded expression on Mateo's face. Normally, Aldo would've made fun of his brother. He didn't because he knew they wore twin expressions.

After their whisper session, Kailyn disentangled herself from her sister. She came up to Aldo and stood with her hands on her hips as she regarded him. He could tell when she'd made a decision and her head bobbed in a nod. Then she stepped closer to him, came up on her tiptoes, and pressed a light kiss to his cheek.

It startled him, but Aldo decided he liked it. Nowhere near as much as he liked kissing her sister. But he'd let Kailyn buss him on the cheek anytime she'd like.

"Hurt her again, and I'll paint your chest hairs with turpentine. Mkay?"

Aldo could only grin at the girl he'd always seen

as the quiet, docile twin. Kailyn reached behind her for Mateo's hand. Mateo had clearly heard her threat because he grinned his approval before walking out the front door with her.

Aldo followed Elayne into the kitchen. He had to make himself take a seat at the island and not stand behind her as she worked over the pots and pans. He constantly had to talk himself down from leaping over the island, snatching her around the waist, and taking her lips as dessert before dinner even finished cooking.

No one was more surprised than him when his resolve lasted long enough for Elayne to put the meal on serving plates. The roasted chicken with garlic potatoes and steamed broccoli made his mouth water. But nowhere near as much as the cook did.

"I have news," said Elayne as she sipped at her glass of wine. "I got offered a new position in the guidance office."

Aldo set down his knife and fork and reached for her hand. He mirrored Elayne's posture, pushing his shoulders back and lifting his chin high. He couldn't be prouder of her.

"We're probably going to have to fake our wedding now."

Aldo's hold on her fingers went lax. His chin dipped. She must have read the question in his eyes.

"Because only our family knows our wedding has already happened, and how. It's not a good look if the townsfolk know that the woman in charge of their children's mental health and career guidance eloped on a drunken bender. Everyone will expect a wedding."

"You want to marry me?"

"Not... I mean... Not, like, this weekend or anything. I thought we could just keep dating for now and tell people we're planning for a ceremony next year or something."

"Next year?"

"I mean, unless we kill each other." She winked at him. "Besides, I would like to actually remember my wedding."

Aldo opened his mouth, then immediately closed it. The truth was on the tip of his tongue. He knew he'd have to tell her, eventually. Otherwise, she was going to find out and be blindsided.

A blindside would hurt her, and he swore he'd never allow any hurt to come to her. This was going to sting, but he had to believe they'd get through it. The worst she could do was yell at him. And that had never bothered him before.

"We're not married."

Elayne threw her head back and laughed. Oh, did that laugh rain down over his heart and soothe him? Though she wasn't taking his words seriously, she still hadn't let go of his hand. Not until she sobered and saw that he hadn't cracked a smile.

Her fingers stiffened in his hand. Then she began to pull them away. It was the fight of his life to loosen his hold.

CHAPTER TWENTY

The day called for rain. At least that's what the meteorologist had said when Elayne had turned the television on as she'd gotten dressed in the morning. It had been overcast for just the first fifteen minutes after she'd stepped outside before work. The sun had shone bright all afternoon, but the rain clouds remained in view in the distance all day long.

"Say that again?" Elayne's voice was calm, as gentle as water lapping on a sandy beach.

She heard the sound of Aldo's throat working. The throaty swallow, was that a nervous gulp? She'd never known the man to be uneasy a day in his life.

Definitely not with her. But there it was—a

quiver at the corner of his lips. A twitch in his right eye.

"When I came over to you at the bar that night, you were drunk and sad. You thought no one wanted to marry you."

The first patter of rain fell against the windowpane. It obscured Elayne's view of the patch of flowers her mother had planted on the day their adoption was made final. She lifted her gaze to Aldo's face and had to blink once to bring him into focus.

"I said I did. I wanted to marry you, and then I gave you my mother's ring. But you never agreed to marry me."

Elayne blinked a few more times, but it did nothing to bring the vision of that night into focus. What was clear was the sound of Aldo's voice. Elayne remembered him saying the words, but she didn't remember the expression he'd worn on his face while doing so.

Aldo Matthews had a special talent for delivering stinging putdowns, all with a straight face. Or worse, his words would rip someone to shreds while wearing that devilishly handsome smirk. His lips were forever lifted in that impish grin that would silently cut Elayne to shreds when he bullied her.

Had he been smirking when he'd said those words to her when she had been at a low point?

"So it was all a joke?" Elayne's voice was still a quiet storm, even as the rain outside picked up. Droplets tapped at the window like they wanted to be let inside.

"It wasn't a joke."

The ferocity in his voice made Elayne blink a few more times, but she couldn't bring him into focus. Somehow the rain had made its way inside and was trailing down her face. Aldo opened his arms and aimed his big, warm body at her.

There was no triumphant smirk on his face. His features fell like he knew his defeat was imminent. But like the stubborn fool that he was, he wasn't giving up.

"You were drunk."

"So you took advantage of me."

"I took you to my room and stayed there with you. I didn't want to leave..." He closed his eyes and inhaled, lines formed in the grooves of his forehead as though the memory was painful. "I couldn't leave. So I stayed and watched you sleep."

"You lied."

It was the only thing Elayne could see clearly.

She certainly couldn't trust her ears. The sincerity and contrition she heard in his voice had to be false. Especially not with her eyes watering the way they were. She swiped at her cheeks before continuing.

"I still can't understand the point of it. What do you get out of pretending to be my husband? Just…" She hiccuped. "Just to ridicule me?"

Arms came around her then and Elayne felt too tired to fight it. She wanted to push him away, to punch him in the chest. But if she did that, he would definitely stop holding her. And she needed to be held, just for a minute, while the world was so blurry.

"What I got out of it was you," he said. "What I wanted out of it was you. I've only ever wanted you."

Elayne shook her head. She couldn't believe those words. Not when she'd seen the exact opposite.

"For more than half my life, you've made fun of me, called me names, and tormented me." When she squirmed, Aldo held on tighter.

"Because it was the only way you would talk to me." His voice was low in her ear. "I tried to be nice to you that first day we met when we were kids. You turned your nose up at me like I was trash."

That wasn't how Elayne remembered it. Aldo had been making fun of another kid, his soon-to-be-brother Topher. Then he'd turned that attention on her and made fun of her hair. Once again, she couldn't believe what he was telling her, not when she had the memories to back up the truth of it.

"I was fascinated by your hair," he said, using one hand to stroke his fingers through her strands. "I called you *Red,* and you shot daggers at me."

No. No, that wasn't how it happened at all. Was it?

"After that, you became my nemesis, and I fell for you."

Elayne pulled away from him. "That's not what that word means."

"You're the goddess who brought me to my knees."

It was an utter downpour outside. A crackle of thunder split the silence between the two of them. Elayne loved a good thunderstorm. She would curl up in a comfy chair with a blanket, a warm cup of tea, and a book. She wanted to forgo the book and tea and use Aldo as a blanket.

But she couldn't.

"You still lied to me about being married."

"No, I didn't. I asked you to marry me. I put a ring on your finger. You and everyone else assumed—"

"You"—Elayne pointed an accusing finger at him—"lied."

He inhaled, holding her gaze. There was so much in that gaze. Defiance, resignation, hope. But she wouldn't be swayed by it.

Elayne couldn't abide liars. She needed all the information to make a decision. The counseling team had kept her in the dark and not included her in on decisions that would affect her job and her livelihood. And now Aldo, the man who had snuck in and stolen her heart, had bald-face lied to her. With him not telling her the information she needed, that would definitely put her job and her livelihood in jeopardy.

"Let's do it," he said.

"Do what?"

"Let's get married."

"Are you insane?"

"Of course I'm insane. I've been in love with a woman who can't stand me since I was a kid. You would never talk to me or look at me without ripping into me, and I came back for more each and every day that I could lay my eyes on you."

Another rumble of thunder crackled between them. The sound of the rain changed. The droplets were no longer banging against the window. The storm was moving on.

Elayne turned away from Aldo. She crossed her arms and hugged herself tightly. She needed to lean on something because her head was spinning around and around. She pressed her lips together to keep herself from screaming or crying.

"Don't do that," he said. "Don't turn away from me. Don't stop talking to me."

She would not let her lip tremble. She would not cry in front of him. "I need to think."

"Think out loud. Talk to me."

"I can't do that. Not when I can't trust that you'll tell me the truth."

"I have never once in my life lied to you."

"But you also didn't tell me everything, did you?"

Not the truth about their relationship status. Not the truth about his feelings.

Aldo inhaled again, but no words came out. There was a part of Elayne that wanted him to fight. Wanted him to get in her face, to shout her down and argue every point that she made with that devil may care smirk in tow. Except this time, she wanted him to care.

Instead, those massive shoulders that had offered her comfort in the storm slumped. He hung his head as though the thunder had struck him in the back. The light in his eyes went out now that the rain had moved on. He looked past her at the back door.

Elayne's heart pounded in her chest. She was angry, but not enough for him to leave. But she couldn't open her mouth to say so. The man she never had any trouble arguing with. She couldn't say anything to him.

It appeared he couldn't say anything to her. Slowly, he turned on his heel and walked to the door.

Her heart thudded when he put his hand on the knob. Her gut wrenched when he turned it with a flick of his wrist. She felt the cold of the rainstorm seep into her bones when he closed the door behind him.

CHAPTER TWENTY-ONE

"You haven't said anything all day."

Aldo got the impression that his brother had been speaking to him for a long time. That beginning of his sentence sounded like it had come in the middle of a longer discussion. But Aldo hadn't been in the mood to have any kind of discussions when he got home last night. He was even less inclined this morning. Why would he talk when the one person he wanted to talk to had stopped talking to him?

If they'd still been kids, Aldo would've marched over to the school and lain in wait until Elayne rounded the corner of the study hall and pounced. Or he could've gone up to the student government offices and casually bumped into her when she came out with her index cards all in order. The time he'd done that, the cards had gone all over the place and were out of order. They'd argued a good ten minutes while he'd helped her gather them up and put them back in order.

If he could go back, he'd toss those note cards aside and pull her to him. He would take a handful of that red hair and tug her closer to him. She would be shocked and indignant, but he would have her full attention.

And that's all he wanted: her attention, her closeness. To feel her mouth pressed against his, whether she made words or not. He knew the exact shape her lips would make. He knew exactly how he would press his mouth against her and taste the shape of her, the texture of her, every-thing about her.

"Al?"

Aldo looked up at his brother. Into the face that was so like his. There was concern etched on Mateo's features. Beneath that concern was joy.

Mateo had won the heart of the woman he loved. He hadn't proposed to Kailyn, not yet. But when he did, there was no doubt that she would say yes. And it wouldn't take a disgusting mix of chocolate and alcohol for her to do it. It was clear in the way that Mateo and Kailyn looked at each other. In how she always reached for him. In how he was always waiting to receive her touch.

Was that where Aldo had gone wrong? Should he have been gentler with Elayne? Maybe he shouldn't have tugged on her hair. Maybe he should've whispered soft words to her all these years.

But no. He'd tried that and failed. Arguing was the only thing that kept her close to him. He was just too tired to do that with her anymore.

"I don't know what to do," Aldo finally admitted.

Mateo didn't ask the obvious question. *About what?* Even if the two of them didn't have the twin-sense between them, it was clear to anyone looking at Aldo that he was heartsick.

"I just want to be with her," he admitted. "When I'm not… everything hurts."

Aldo scratched at his chest, but it didn't lessen the ache inside. His head throbbed from trying to work out the best angle to approach her and coming up empty. His eyes stung from being wide open all night long. His fingertips were numb from being clenched into fists at his side as he tried to hold himself still and not race back to her house and bang on the door to be let in, to be let close to her.

"Have you told her that?" asked Mateo. "She might like to know you're in pain."

The laugh hurt his throat as it pushed out of raw lungs. But it felt good. Sitting out on the back patio with his brothers felt good. Charlie sat in their dad's creaky rocking chair, rubbing his thumb and index finger on his chin in the same way their father had done when they asked him for advice.

"Don't give up, bro," said Charlie. "It took me and Savy two decades before we finally got our forever."

"Until you got your forever?" Topher scoffed from his place, sitting on the steps. "You sound just like her. What's next? You'll be singing show tunes while you sweep the kitchen floor."

Charlie took off his hat and tossed it down the stairs. The assault only got a chuckle out of Topher as he snatched the hat out of the air and flung it back at Charlie.

"I wasn't going to give up," Aldo said. "I just don't know how to fight this battle."

"Statistically, you shouldn't fight," said Joe as he

leaned against the railing. "With each of our relationships, we chased after the women, but it wasn't until they stopped running and marched up to us that the battle was over."

"Are you telling him to give up?" Will asked from his cross-legged position on the ground. There was a pen in his hand, a pad of paper in his lap. Mateo couldn't see the words, but he was certain Will was working on a poem that his wife Tricksy would take to the studio and turn into another hit song.

"I'm not saying give up," said Joe. "Just stop fighting. She'll come back to you when she's ready."

"Did Foxy say something to you?" Aldo asked hopefully. Joe's psychic wife had seen each of their relationships unfolding before they got underway. But Foxy's visions, or rather her clairsentience, weren't perfect. She was only right half the time.

"She saw that you two were married when you got back home from your trip," said Joe.

"But they weren't married," said Mateo.

Foxy had gotten that part wrong. Aldo had proposed, and he'd meant it. He wanted to spend the rest of his life with Elayne. Fighting with her, making up with her, doing all manner of things to that expressive mouth of hers.

"You need to march over there and let her know what's what," Topher said as he rose from his place on the steps. "Demand to see her. Demand that she listen."

"And how would Toni react to that?" Charlie asked as he rocked back in the chair, his mouth quirked in the same way as when their father decided to let one of his sons touch the fire to see how hot it was. Metaphorically speaking—mostly.

"She'd take my head off." Topher grinned as he scratched the back of his head. "But at least I'd have her hands on me."

Aldo liked Topher's idea the best. He'd let Elayne pound on him, yell at him, do anything she wanted to him. Just so long as he had her with him.

Her wrath he could stand. He'd been doing that for years. It was her silence, her absence, that would break him.

In the end, Aldo decided to compromise. He would give Elayne some space for the rest of the day while he was at the police academy training. Then he would go and pound on her door.

When he took his seat in class, he was gratified to know that they had added a new cadet to the program. The town was growing, and it would need a lot more officers to ensure its citizens were safe. Aldo would help with recruiting once he got himself situated on the force. Any and everything to keep Elayne safe, especially if he couldn't be with her all the time.

For the next four hours, Aldo managed to keep Elayne off his mind. Mostly. The knowledge that everything he was learning would be put in use to protect her and keep her safe allowed him to focus on the lessons at hand. As they were packing up to leave for the day, Chief Moss poked his head in the door.

He shook hands with the other cadets and asked after their health and their progress. When he got to Aldo, he placed a strong grip on Aldo's shoulder. The older man's smile broadened, reminding Aldo of his biological father's grin.

Aldo had been a bit of a hellion growing up. But both of his fathers had each seen past that to the man he would become. Standing in front of Chief Moss, a man who had been at the crossroads when Aldo could've gone down the wrong path, that approving head nod was confirmation that Aldo had made all the right choices in his life, and the chief recognized it.

"The missus and I are having some friends over for dinner tonight," said Chief. "I know it's short notice, but I'd love for you and your fiancée to join us."

Aldo opened his mouth, but the words stuck in his throat. He was that snot-nosed kid staring down two potential paths. Except this time, he wasn't the only one his decisions would affect. He knew exactly which road he was supposed to take. He just didn't know how his decision would affect the woman he loved.

"Elayne isn't my fiancée, sir."

"No?"

"She didn't say yes when I proposed."

"She's been wearing your ring."

"She couldn't get it off her finger at first."

"Well, that's a sign if ever I saw one," Chief Moss chuckled.

"I misled her. Not when I proposed, but…"

Aldo let the sentence die. He couldn't see a way to explain that he'd proposed to Elayne when she was drunk, and then spent a platonic night with her, only to wake up in the morning and not correct her when she thought they'd actually gotten married. Hearing it that way made him see why Elayne was a bit miffed.

"The problem is, I'd do it again." Aldo tilted his head back and looked out the window at the cloudless sky. "All I've ever wanted was to be close to that woman."

"Then you should come with me. There's something I think you should see."

CHAPTER TWENTY-TWO

Elayne sat in the meeting room at the school board. It was supposed to be her day, the one she'd been working toward for years. She felt nothing but a hollow ache in her chest.

"Tell us about yourself, Mrs...." Ted Heath, who had been hired a year after Elayne, looked down again at the stack of papers set before. "I beg your pardon, *Miss* Jade."

Elayne couldn't even muster a single huff of anger at the man. She was all tapped out of the emotion. Even if she could get upset, she wouldn't waste it on the likes of the tall, thin man whose wedding ring kept slipping up and down his boney left ring finger.

He knew her. All of the men and women sitting

across the table knew her. This was the first time they'd actually paid attention to her. And it was all because of the ring on her finger.

Elayne glanced down at the ring. She'd tried to tug it off again last night. The ring held fast. She had to admit that her attempts had been half-hearted. The ring had become a comfort sitting on her finger instead of a vise.

"I'm not married," she said in answer to Ted's question.

All around the table, pencils stopped waggling around on paper. Gazes came up and looked at her. But not really seeing her.

Dr. Moss was the first to recover her smile. She poked the eraser tip of her pencil at Elayne's left hand. "Not yet, but I hope you're planning for a spring wedding. I do love spring weddings."

"I don't know if there's going to be a wedding. I didn't agree to the proposal." Elayne rolled the band around her finger. It was looser than it had been. Using her thumb, she tucked the ring snuggly down toward her knuckles. "But I want to marry him."

Around the table, the other counselors shuffled and fidgeted. Once again, Dr. Moss was the first to speak up.

"None of this matters, Elayne. Whether you accepted Mr. Matthews' proposal at first or later—"

"But it does matter. Because none of you took me or my ideas seriously until he put this ring on my finger."

Elayne held her hand up as evidence. The diamond twinkled at her. It reminded her of the look in Aldo's eyes, the look when he'd asked her to marry him under the dim lights of a bar.

"I would never do anything to hurt you, Elayne," he'd said. "Let me prove it. Take my ring."

He had asked her to marry him. He hadn't smirked or scoffed. There had been vulnerability in those hazel eyes of his. There had been hope and desire. Because he wanted her.

"I didn't say yes," Elayne said to the room of confused peers. "He said he'd spend his days proving he's the one for me."

A few sighs from the women in the room brought Elayne back to the present moment. Dr. Moss had a soft smile on her face. Ted looked on the verge of annoyed. Elayne didn't care. She rose from the seat.

"Where are you going? We're not done here." Ted pointed to his list of questions.

"I proved I'm the one for this job on my first day. If you all need more proof than that, then I'm not the one. But I need to go and find my one."

"What?" said Ted, his gaze connecting to the two other men in the room, only one of who wore a similarly baffled expression.

The women dabbed at their eyes. One of the women who had been here since Elayne was in school gave Elayne a discreet pump of her fist.

"She's right," said Dr. Moss. "The creation of this new position is based on a report Ms. Jade wrote. She knows the role inside and out. This interview is just a formality. The job is yours."

Dr. Moss rose and reached across the table, extending her hand.

Elayne hesitated. Not because she wasn't sure if she wanted the job or not. She did. But she wanted to get out of this room and find Aldo to tell him how she truly felt. But there was no reason she couldn't have both her man and the promotion. Elayne took Dr. Moss' hand.

"The job is yours regardless of your marital status," said Dr. Moss. "But if you're a smart woman, you'll lock that Matthews boy down. I've seen the way he looks at you."

Elayne let herself see the things she'd never

seen in Aldo's eyes as she replayed the words he'd said to her over the last few days.

I've never hated you. You decided you didn't like me.

I like you, Elayne Jade. You're the smartest girl I know.

If she was so smart, how come she was so dumb? How could she not see that none of the words out of his mouth had been said in hatred? How had she not seen that quirk in his smile when he faced off with her? It was all so obvious now.

Are you asking me to marry you?

Yes.

You think I'll say yes?

No. Not yet. But maybe one day. Until that day, I'm going to prove I'm the one for you.

That was it. That's when it happened. She'd fallen for Aldo Matthews, and it had taken a cocktail of alcohol and chocolate to make her see the truth.

"I'm gonna go and lock that down. I'm going to marry that man. But I have to propose to him first."

CHAPTER TWENTY-THREE

"Come sit with your family, son."

Sitting was the last thing Aldo wanted to do. He was itching to go find Elayne. When he and Captain Moss had arrived at the Board of Education where they were holding her interview, the room had been empty. Aldo hadn't waited for Moss to call his wife to see where they might've taken Elayne for a celebratory meal or drink. He'd started his hunt.

She wasn't at her house. She wasn't at the school. Kailyn, who sat in the cradle of Mateo's arms, didn't know where she was either. She wasn't picking up any calls or answering texts. Aldo was starting to worry.

"I need to find her, Dad."

"I understand, son. Just nourish yourself first. It's the first time we've all been together under the same roof for years."

By all, Father Matthews didn't just mean all six of his sons. All wives, fiancées, and girlfriends were here as well. So was the other half of their family. The six Silver sisters and their husbands were also gathered in the yard, filling out two picnic tables. And then there were the five foster kids who were all officially adopted and now proper Matthewses.

But his father's words weren't exactly true. They weren't all together. One person was missing.

Aldo stood up to defy his father and leave when the sound of a car kicking up dirt down the drive had him turning. He knew it was her before his body came completely around. There was no one else unaccounted for.

He ran down the lane to meet her to a chorus of cheers from his brothers, sisters-in-law, Silver sisters, and fellow brothers-in-love. Aldo barely waited for the car to come to a stop before yanking the driver's side door open, lifting her out, and pulling her into his arms.

He had no clue whether she was there for him or not. He had no idea if she'd deck him for being so forward, and he didn't care. She was right where she belonged: in his arms.

"Where have you been?" he shouted as he pulled back.

"I was looking for you," she shouted right back at him.

"I was looking for you." Aldo hadn't let her go. They were still pressed together from their knees to their chests. But they glared into each other's faces. "Why didn't you answer your phone?"

"Because I was driving around looking for you." Elayne's cheeks were flushed and red as she pursed her lips and gave Aldo her death stare.

"Well, that was smart." His hands clenched into the back of her dress. "It's not safe to text and drive."

"I know." Her nostrils flared as she shoved her hand against his chest, right over his heart.

The organ gave a kick, like it was a puppy who'd just gotten its first scratch behind the ears. "I love you."

Elayne threw her arms around his neck and locked down. "I love you, too."

She hadn't cold-cocked him in the jaw, but it was enough to knock him backward. He was done with the shouting and fighting. He had a better plan for those expressive lips of hers. Like the warrior he'd been trained to be, Aldo stormed in and captured Elayne's mouth.

She didn't put up any protest. She hugged him tighter than he knew she had the strength to do. She pressed herself into him, giving herself fully to him. Her fingers tugged at the strands of his hair, and he knew exactly what that meant.

"I'm sorry," he said when he let her up for breath.

At the same time as she said, "I'm sorry."

"What did you do?"

"The same thing I've always done to you: I didn't listen. I misjudged you. I walked away instead of talking it out. And I'm sorry."

Aldo shrugged, burying his nose in those red strands that had always fascinated him. "I don't care, as long as I've got your attention."

"I'm going to be nice to you from now on."

"Why?" He pulled back, staring down at her in utter disbelief. "I mean, sure, if you want to."

"I'm trying to give a grand gesture." She smacked him on the shoulder.

Aldo captured her hand and kissed her fingers. "You're doing it beautifully, love."

Elayne curled her fingers. She looked down,

chewing at the inside of her mouth. She looked vulnerable, uncertain. Aldo tightened his hold.

"I have something to ask you," she said finally.

"The answer is yes."

Her small smile was only half amused, and then the uncertainty came back. "Listen to me."

Aldo made a show of sobering his expression. But she had to know that he was telling her the truth. Whatever she asked him, the answer would be yes.

From the picnic tables, there was silence in the peanut gallery. Forks were abandoned. Even the kids were quiet as they watched the final soap opera across the Silver Star and Flying Cross ranches play out.

"You asked me a question," Elayne said. "I couldn't remember it before. Until today."

He nodded, holding his breath. Had she remembered the night he'd proposed to her? He wanted to know exactly what she remembered. But it looked like she'd gotten the highlights.

"I called you a nightmare."

Aldo shrugged again. "Close enough to an endearment for me, my love."

"You're not a nightmare. You're my hero."

"Well, you are my nemesis. It's the least I can do."

She shook her head, but the uncertainty was gone. Aldo decided he'd spend the rest of his life trying to replicate that smile. When her lips stretched broad, it was so much better than the M of upset. Much easier access for kissing, too.

"Aldo, I came here to propose to you."

"You know that's the man's job."

"Hey!" She smacked his shoulder.

"But I'm an evolved man. So ask me."

"Quit bossing me around, Matthews."

"You think I'll say yes?"

"Oh, please! You are so into me."

"It's true. I am."

Elayne opened her mouth to say more, but Aldo had already heard everything he needed to hear. Her lips were stretched in another smile, and it was past time he knew what that expression on Elayne Jade tasted like. So he dove in.

Shanae Johnson was raised by Saturday Morning cartoons and After School Specials. She still doesn't understand why there isn't a life lesson that ties the issues of the day together just before bedtime. While she's still waiting for the meaning of it all, she writes stories to try and figure it all out. Her books are wholesome and sweet, but her are heroes are hot and heroines are full of sass!

And by the way, the E elongates the A. So it's pronounced Shan-aaaaaaaa. Perfect for a hero to call out across the moors, or up to a balcony, or to blare outside her window on a boombox. If you hear him calling her name, please send him her way!

You can sign up for Shanae's Reader Group and receive a FREE NOVELLA in this world at

https://shanaejohnson.com/ReaderGroup

ALSO BY SHANAE JOHNSON

a Flying Cross Ranch Romance
His Vow to Love

His Vow to Treasure

His Vow to Adore

His Vow to Trust

His Vow to Respect

His Vow to Defend

The Silver Star Ranch Romances

His Pledge to Honor

His Pledge to Cherish

His Pledge to Protect

His Pledge to Obey

His Pledge to Have

His Pledge to Hold

The Brides of Purple Heart

On His Bended Knee

Hand Over His Heart

Offering His Arm

His Permanent Scar

Having His Back

In Over His Head

Always On His Mind

Every Step He Takes

In His Good Hands

Light Up His Life

Strength to Stand

His Grace Under Pressure

The Rangers of Purple Heart

The Rancher takes his Convenient Bride

The Rancher takes his Best Friend's Sister

The Rancher takes his Runaway Bride

The Rancher takes his Star Crossed Love

The Rancher takes his Love at First Sight

The Rancher takes his Last Chance at Love